A little LOVE incident

...and accidentlly a love story

By the same author

My Love never facked...
As Long as I Love you...

A little LOVE incident

...and accidentlly a love story

Nikhil Mahajan • Aakhyaa Pandey

Srishti
PUBLISHERS & DISTRIBUTORS

SRISHTI PUBLISHERS & DISTRIBUTORS
N-16, C. R. Park
New Delhi 110 019
srishtipublishers@gmail.com

First published by Srishti Publishers & Distributors in 2012

Typeset in AGaramond 12pt. by Suresh Kumar Sharma at Srishti

Dear Destiny, I am a writer now...

Acknowledgements

FROM NIKHIL: I would like to thank my "Bade Papa" to strengthen my thoughts with his wise advice. Here I am thanking my little' sweet gf' again and always because she inspires me to write, and I admit because of her– I am a writer.

I would also like to thank my mates Akhil, Amit, Aman, Jai, Prashant, Sunil, Vikram and Varun for making a family more than friends.

For my co-author AAKHYAA: My favorite gal, she has something magical in her, which sprouts a good person in you. And I am really thankful to her to undertake this venture. This story could never have been completed without Aakhyaa's presence and contribution.

FROM AAKHYAA: This book is my first attempt to satisfy the appetite of those who love to imbibe the pleasure of reading beautiful stories based on very special relationships that develop from simple conversations.

From my side, I wish to thank my Dad from whom I inherit these genes of writing, and my mom who always stopped me from reading novels, which further increased my urge to read more of them. A token of gratitude to my brother - Aman who was by my side in all my good and tough times of my life. And my friends in alphabetical order – Aastha, Farhaan, Fizza, Jyoti, Namrata, Pranay, Salmaan, Shashank, Shraddha, Shubhangi, Sourav. All of you deserve loads of thanks.

And last but not the least, special thanks to you readers for choosing this book to read. Hope you enjoy the roller coaster ride of the characters and their unusual and unique story.

For my co-author NIKHIL: This book in your hand would have been just a dream without Mahajan, who is the ultimate source of all the inspiration and motivation for all the woven threads of thoughts, an imagination converted into a beautiful and colorful story.

Together: We would like to thank our readers for giving us immense strength when they cherish our writing. And of course, our critics who are the real friends.

We would like to thank our **editor** for giving a promising hand to our venture, brushing it up and polishing it with his wise suggestions.

Thanks to all those who discouraged; all the way strengthening us to work on a project like this.

Foreward

The best days of our life are the vexatious periods that make you wise with each catch; we blame others for our problems, but never consider our strings being controlled by destiny. The journey of a Physiotherapist, a loser in love and continuing a relationship stepping into the shoes of a successful writer was at no time been so smooth. People were always interested to know what happened further to the protagonists Abhi and Mani namely me in the books. The story goes back to the incidents that took place in the previous books of mine. However, with the final editing, they were eventually eliminated and now as life after the book has changed, the unfinished work is still on the cards. This was the purpose of rewriting this book of my life, my so-called "**fcukkn* autobiography ....**"

NIKHIL: Life is like a church bell, it always says *bajaate raho*. As I look at my life, I find I am a loser left empty handed. My life and thoughts orbit loving a girl, but for her, I knew it was never me. I have never been so fortunate and my friend always says: "You need more breakups and hookups for your readers." Here I am again with a new manuscript, a story, **A LITTLE LOVE INCIDNT... & ACCIDENTALLY TURNING IT INTO A BOOK.**

AAKHYAA: My friend talked about the *bajaate raho* funda, well my friendship starts with Nikhil from a *bajaate raho* incident that you will read in the subsequent chapters of this book. I would like to mention his idiotic love story (well I love to say it *SILLY-JILLY*) titled MY LOVE NEVER FAKED as he says nothing is complete without it. The story starts with the protagonist named *Abhi* as Nikhil himself with the name changed. He wrote this book for his girlfriend, something I found an archaic thing one can do for someone. It was weird to hear that she came back after reading his book. Huh. Keeping close to the story, Nikhil *as Abhi* was always making disastrous mistakes in his life because of his malicious attitude and Priya; his Gf had constantly forgiven him for all this. She used to say that one day she would leave him if things went on like that. However, being careless, he never thought that Priya would ever leave him but later somehow Ellen, a beautiful American woman, came in between them to whom, Abhi got distracted and confused. As always, he kept his mistakes on priority so finally Priya broke off from him. He wrote this book for Priya: "my love never faked..." supposed to be a story about two hearts beating as one. Two "I" so-called "we"; A cute story of love between two hearts beating for one reason called "together." Two "I" so called "we" What a fuck! But do you think something like this can happen?

NIKHIL: Well not digressing from the subject and the book, let's move to a little love incident.

{A pretty girl is like a melody
That haunts you night and day}

-Irving Berlin

CHAPTER 1
FROM AAKHYAA'S PEN:

A few months ago, I was struggling with my relationship. It was a difficult time. I was an excellent student, in love with a stupid boy from my class. I did well in school and considered myself attractive as well; it is a wonder how I fell in love with a guy who barely scored average marks in my class. He was unimpressive except for a gorgeous smile and witty jokes. According to my classmates, he was by far the most attractive boy in our class. Though most girls spent a lot of time drooling over him, I had only recently noticed him. It was by chance that he became my boyfriend when he announced his feelings for me unexpectedly.

It was a free period, and everyone in the class was in a mood of masti. Suddenly …

"Would you be my girlfriend?" asked Shobhit strangely and unexpectedly.

He was on his knees with a flower in his hand. I felt very embarrassed with him asking me such a question in front of the whole class. He was a backbencher attempting to conquer the territory and the heart of a first bencher. In my heart and mind that was a far nicer attempt as compared to his standards but the timing was terribly wrong. He remained kneeling on the floor with the flower in the hand, and I looked at him with an expressionless face. The whole class was cheering for his ridiculously daring act. I was absolutely confused and too shocked to react to his question, yet he remained on his knees obviously enjoying the attention and waiting for my reply. I began gathering my things into my bag, planning my escape from this brazen and stubborn boy. All the boys in the room were waving at him, and he was smiling back at them, with his flirtatious smile, all the while everyone in the class was screaming and shouting my name loudly, poking fun at the spectacle.

Shobhit was a cool guy, but he was always in some kind of trouble; the idea that he would genuinely ask such a question was absurd. This was not his character at all.

"Why you are not replying to me? I am waiting for your answer." asked Shobhit again.

"I give you two options here." continued Shobhit with his collar popped up and school tie undone and his shirt out.

"Yes or *haan*, choose whatever you wish." he continued.

I still could not say anything. Suddenly, all the noise around us stopped as a teacher entered the classroom wondering about the noise. Before I could move my hand to take his flower and give him an answer, the teacher removed us from the classroom.

I was now his partner in crime; I had never been yelled at so much. We were taken out of the class to the principal. Shobhit was fortunate that we were partners in the trouble; the principal knew that I was a good student and did not punish us severely. We were told to stand outside his office for the next two hours. After an hour passed, Shobhit broke the silence.

"You didn't answer me sweetie." Shobhit used the same shameless tone as before.

"This is no joke Shobhit; we are in trouble."

"When am I not in trouble?" smiled Shobhit, his carefree nature and smile convinced me of his confidence and sincerity.

That was the first time I had noticed how different Shobhit was from the other guys in my class.

That day I noticed that he was way different from rest of guys around. I was an intelligent girl with 99% marks and always busy studying for that 1%, but it was Shobhit, who was the 1% missing in my life.

A few months later, after my board exams I finally accepted Shobhit's proposal and we went out for a date.

"The boards are over! What a relief!" I said to Shobhit.

"Yes Baby, I am feeling relaxed now. This last month had been terrible. What grade are you expecting sweetie?" he asked.

"Well I guess an 89% this time." I answered as I looked out of the window; I knew it was a sad moment because from this point we would be entering the real world.

"Ahem! Great, I think I am going to fail in math." he said disappointed.

I was little stunned but for a backbencher to say such a thing was quite common. I trusted Shobhit, and I cared for his grades; I wanted him to fail.

"Don't talk like rubbish Shobhit, you will make it through." I tried to comfort and assure him.

"Leave it. Let's not talk about school, not while we are on a date," Shobhit gave a smile.

"Would you like to eat something else?" he asked trying to change the topic.

"Nope! I am full," I answered as I didn't want to ruin a perfect date stuffing myself.

"Okay! We should get some exercise, to help digest the food. Let's have some fun" said Shobhit excitingly. He was ready to take me to an amusement park. He took me by the hand and dragged me to one of his favorite amusement rides. This was his favorite because it was a fast one and boy like speed, especially when seeking an opportunity to sit close to their girlfriend. He knew that this was his chance because I was easily frightened by high speed and would cling to him as he had planned. As the speed of the ride increased my arms around him began to get tighter, and he really enjoyed it. Even with all the gravitational laws on our body, our hearts still beat to the law of attraction.

As the ride slowed and my feet were finally on the ground, my mind still felt as if it was under the influence of the G-forces on the ride, Shobhit held me so that I would not fall down. His caresses were very enjoyable. As we moved a little away from the ride, he came close to me and caressed my hair while looking into my eyes. His gaze was long and intense; he said, "**You know, you complete me.**" Shobhit was very romantic, and he had spoken what I had been thinking all along. I was very happy to find that Shobhit thought the same.

"Let's dance in the water!" I shouted in excitement as I heard my favorite song playing on a radio and people singing along. He kissed me gently, but I was not distracted. I took his hand, and we ran towards the pool.

After a few hours of dancing in the water; hugging each other and enjoying each other's warmth it was late so we got out of the pool. On the way back home it was all calm and quiet, when we had to leave each other. My eyes were full of tears, even though neither of us said anything. Finally, he broke the silence and asked me, "Where are you planning to study after you receive your exam results?"

"Mom and Dad are planning to send me to Kota for medical coaching."

"And what do you want?" He wanted to know my point of view.

"I want to go to Kota." I replied.

"Has it been decided? Shobhit asked again to confirm.

"Yes, almost" I replied with excitement.

"I have heard it's heaven for the aspiring medical students." I gave a smile along with my googled answer.

"***Great baby!*** I wish you all the luck I know you will be a successful doctor but remember that I must be your first patient." Shobhit joked.

"Shut up Shobhit." I replied

"I don't think I will be okay without you." Shobhit had a romantic and wistful tone this time.

"What are your plans?" I questioned.

"I plan to miss you, *jaan*." he could not shake off his romantic mood.

"I am seriously worried for you. Why are you not serious about your career?" I asked, frustrated.

"I don't know much." Shobhit replied.

"Still, there must be something you have planned." I asked for the last time. This was the worst thing about Shobhit. He had no plan for his life and we had already fought bitterly on this issue.

"Maybe I will join the army to Noida to pursue BBA. I'll be leaving to get my seat reserved." he said.

"I will miss you." he added.

"I will miss you too." I responded quickly so as not to get into the same argument again.

To hear that he would miss me meant the world to me. I still could not believe how quickly our time together had passed.

Finally, I was in front of the gate of my building and now it was time for us to say good-bye. I was not feeling good, so before I could say good-bye Shobhit came close to me and kissed me on the forehead. I closed my eyes and expected Shobhit to kiss me on the cheek, but to my surprise he kissed me on the lips. I could not hold myself back, so I began to kiss him back as he caressed my back.

"No one is at home." I said offering him an opportunity to share himself with me.

"Should I visit your bedroom?" he asked.

"No, visit my heart baby." I shot back.

I allowed him into my home and into my heart. We made love for the first time, it was perfect. I kissed him good-bye as he left right before my parents arrived home.

As we met for another day

The heart beats fast and I just pray

Kisses on the cheeks

With a hand shake

You gift me your soul with

A bunch of flowers and the cake

To make it more purposeful

I kiss you and wish this time to stay

Then I made a way into the bed

Here our hotness came into play

Hands all over the body and the soul

In the end our body dashed into each other

The first time I felt everything so slowly

Just like a light years

I felt I am complete as I lose it to you

My first man my memory, oh he's all mine

Another day another time

This mind was always just thinking of you

I kiss you and romantically I am all yours

Yours forever

Forever for this life time, rest I know nothing

Now and never...

As we pulled apart from each other, a few days after my first perfect date, there were a few life time scratches Shobhit left for me...

{When I'm not near the girl I love,

I love the girl I'm near}

- E.Y. Harburg

CHAPTER 2

Sunken deep into sweet memories with Shobhit, I lay my bed thinking that there could be nothing better in my life than him. I was extensively in my thoughts when suddenly Shobhit began knocking at my window. I looked outside and I found Shobhit hanging on to my balcony.

"Hey open the window." said Shobhit as he repeatedly knocked on the window pane.

"Shobhit, why are you here at this time of the night?" I asked as I opened the window and let him into my room.

"I am leaving tomorrow and I wanted to tell you the good news in person." said Shobhit as he leaned on me.

"My father helped me get a seat in a much esteemed college." he said dramatically while wrapping his arms around me.

"Congrats." I congratulate him for his success, with my arms around his neck and his nose touching mine.

"Is your stuff packed?" I questioned him like an archetypal girlfriend.

"Yes everything is done, I have just one thing left to do." replied Shobhit giving me a little kiss on my tender pink lips.

"What?" I babbled.

"You baby!" Shobhit came close to me with a smile.

"I want to give you one last hug before I leave." he continued as he clasped his arms very tightly around me, pulling close to his muscular chest. I felt so safe there.

I switched off the light in my room and we lay down near the window on the floor with a pillow under our heads. Here we could see the sky; it was a clear night and the stars were twinkling beautifully. I could see Shobhit's eyes glued on me under the moonlight. The intensity of his gaze was making me burn with passion; I trembled and felt goose bumps beginning to form. I nestled close to him; he hugged me tightly in response; I felt I was being blessed with his hugs and kisses. I felt grand as I found myself blessed with his arms under the moonlight; its beauty was enhanced by millions of stars twinkling like diamonds. He held my hand tightly, and we spoke about our beautiful future as he confessed his deep desire to marry me after finishing college.

"What happens to the time? Why does it slip away so quickly when we are close to each other?" I asked.

"I don't know?" Shobhit said smiling ingenuously.

I wanted to be with him and to make love to him but there was no time. I was already being a little brave with his presence in my room, I allowed him until early morning just before dawn. I was left alone with my books and sweet memories of him haunting my heart. I wished something more could happen between us, but my heart would not let me go where Shobhit wanted.

THE END OF THE START

As Shobhit went to his college, I tried concentrating more on my books and studied as hard as I could, so that I too could meet his expectations. He was my strength and my entire world; I wanted to make him proud. His memories haunted my mind, a day never passed without my thinking of him. Destiny had something else in store for me; the wise always say that life never happens as you plan. It took only a few months before Shobhit settled down at college and I was all broken into pieces because of his absence from my life. To add fuel to the fire, I began to hear rumors that Shobhit had begun dating another girl in his college. I refused to believe the rumors, though they only made me miss him more.

As time passed, I started thinking more and more about him. Nothing came of my thoughts but disappointment and a heart on the point of breaking. Shobhit, the cool guy, was alleged to have been dating beautiful girls along with me. I had never believed these rumors because I had trusted Shobhit and I wished that I would never have to question this.

One cold winter morning, my brother Kartik visited my place. He dashed into my room with anger and as he entered…

"*Di* wake up! You are asleep and my world is upside down!" bawled Kartik.

"Look I am not just your brother; I look out for you too. We share a friendship deeper than just our kinship. I am your best friend and have come to tell you to look into your relationship with Shobhit." he pleaded with me.

Kartik, my younger brother, was someone I trusted more than my boyfriend and his words of confirmation that Shobhit was definitely dating someone had left me heartbroken. I now knew that he was not to be trusted.

I spent weeks crying my heart out, I was totally shattered. Sooner or later you have to realize your mistakes and learn from them, so I did. I tried my best to forget, but I could not. Shobhit managed to beg forgiveness for his mistakes and I gave him a final chance. He never changed and I kept receiving news of his infidelity. I confronted him and we fought for the last time. I wished I could forgive him, but he was not ready to change his ways. Finally, I broke up with him and had to let our relationship go.

One morning I received a book from Shobhit as a gift some kind of justification for his actions. I had expected at least a letter of apology from him, not a romance novel. I put the book on my bookshelf and texted Shobhit to confirm I had received it. It only took a few minutes for Shobhit to message me as his last try to win me over:

From Shobhit - "**Are you reading the book?**"

His text annoyed me. I was confused as to why he was so eager for me to read this book. Why was he trying to persuade me into reading this book when he should have been apologizing for his actions?

To Shobhit - "**I am not interested.**"

I texted him back and opened the book. I wanted to find why Shobhit desired me to read this book. Just flipping the first few pages made me realize that the story seemed similar to my life, it was about a man flirting with many girls just as Shobhit had done.

After a few hours of reading the book furiously:

I wasted four hours of precious study time reading the book that Shobhit had sent to me. The story was chauvinistic to say the least, a story about a man who lived very much as Shobhit had and a woman who had sacrificed herself for an untrustworthy man as I had with Shobhit. The story was the same except for a dramatic reconciliation in the last few lines of the book that required a large stretch of imagination. The woman in the story returns to the man who broke her heart, and I felt like garbage after reading this. Did Shobhit think I was going to take him back after reading this story?

This book was autobiographical, written by a young man named Nikhil Mahajan, a book he had written to confess his misgivings to his ex-girlfriend, just as Shobhit was trying to do with me. Mr. Mahajan expected to receive the last chance to be loved by the woman he adored. The woman replied with forgiveness and tears in her eyes. I wonder why it was the woman crying and not Mr. Mahajan.

As I reached the last chapter of the book, I became more tense and irritated. It had a few filmy and cheesy dialogues like:

"As we lived a life together and we had talked so much to each other ... despite bad conditions..."

"Oh my God what the fuck," I shouted out aloud as I read. I didn't like something like this. After a blunder of mistakes the fucking story had a happy ending. I was confused about the psyche of the author and why he thought people should overlook infidelity and trust the same person again. Again I continued reading the book as it opened to the next few lines:

"There were some bad times we faced and some good times but it never happened that we stopped talking and you had such a bad impression of me your mind." Mr. Mahajan continued repeating these

lines in the book and that made me want to hurt him.

"*Idiot can't you look into my eyes when I confess something. You always make me cry with your words and when I want you to see my loyalty in my eyes you are not interested.*" I was out of my senses after reading this; I knew that any girl in this situation would have left this guy for dead. Mahajan was writing a story that degraded the very girl who took him back graciously. "**Patriarchy**" I said to myself.

Suddenly my mobile beeped and as I looked at its screen there was a message:

From Shobhit - "**Are you reading it?**"

"*Yes, and would you mind doing your own work?*" I texted him back in anger trying to hurt him.

The only question that remained unrequited in my mind; what would this man have done if it was the girl who had betrayed him in the same manner that he betrayed her?

I felt bad for Shobhit as he expected reconciliation after I read the book. I read the book through trying to read between the lines what Shobhit might have wanted me to understand.

The story ended with this line: "*This time I really wanted to tell you that I could understand neither you nor your love for me. As I look for you now, I find nothing wrong with you and if you do not come back to me now I will call myself a loser*" I could not believe that I had read the entire book; my heart began to hate the author.

The title of the book should have been *MY LOVE IS FAKE...*

"*C'mon make a move, hold me in your arms*" As I read this line I threw the book against the wall considering it as a piece of shit and hurried to send a text a message to Shobhit:

"This is bullshit and so is this writer for expecting such a thing"

I knew now that Shobhit was expecting this angry reaction, and this was not in his favor.

A reply text came back in no time:

"Look, this guy got a chance and I deserve one too."

To distract myself, I tried to study my school books but the book that I had thrown across the room, now lying near the door attracted my attention again. I picked it up and read it another time from where I had left up to the last page. I was now very curious to know what happened next. I again continued to read to it...

"*I have two things to say, one is good and the other bad. The good thing is that I am with you! The bad news is how I can be with you?*"

"*If I am not with you I think I will get lost in this big world. It's a large world for people like us. And living a moment without you is like missing a lifetime.*", "**What a loser**" I exclaimed.

But the book keeps on unfolding selfishly for Mahajan: "*She started crying like a baby and just hugged me tightly. I too hugged her and to make her feel better I whispered in her ears. The moment* is changing everything. *I don't know what is happening to us and between us, but when I am with you I feel as if I am home. I promise to be faithful to you for the rest of my life.*" Then Priya, the girl with Mahajan, his girlfriend handed the gift which she had got for him. As Mahajan opened the packet and found his book he could not stop himself from hugging her.

"*Love you always*" said Priya and they kissed each other. He held his girl tight and found his love again.

I finished the book and knew what he expected from this writing. A happy ending that's what I hated most about the love stories. At the end of the story Mahajan strengthened the love story with a happy note:

"*You know, no matter what you do, if you have a true love in your life, someone who also loves you that much … he will be with you always.*"

---------@---------

"LOVE NEVER FADES…"

Story ends but Love never ends….

I was very angry and had great hatred for two people: Nikhil Mahajan and Shobhit. Shobhit for cheating on me and the writer Nikhil for writing a book that justified cheating.

In a fit of anger I searched for this writer's email and I sent him an email that went something like this:

Subject: I hate you for writing your book.

TO: Mr. Nikhil Mahajan

Mr. Mahajan, I have only two things to say to you. The book you wrote is chauvinistic garbage. You only try to show that it's a man's world; a society where men can do whatever they like and women are expected to sacrifice and forgive their men for all the wrong that they have done. A real relationship is built on trust and love.

Once I had sent the email to Mahajan, I knew my love life with Shobhit could never continue. I texted him for the last time:

"We have broken up, please never think of justifying your actions with the help of this book" I was finally through with him. I emailed Nikhil again, because he did not reply to my message; I was expecting an irate email in reply. I wanted to fight with him as I had fought with Shobhit.

{After great pain, a formal feeling comes,
The Nerves sit ceremonious, like Tombs}

-Emily Dickinson

CHAPTER 3

FROM NIKHIL'S PEN:

From here I will continue with the story. I am Nikhil Mahajan, author of the book *Aakhyaa* just mentioned you. After the huge success of my debut novel titled My Love Never Faked, a national bestseller, there was something still missing from my life and it was Priya's presence. Well being the protagonist (Abhi) in the novel there was something I could not match with him. It was that Priya never cared to come back into my life again as it happened in the novel. Writing novels was a good way to overcome pain and connect with millions of people reading my book every day. I was fading each second but yet living the life of a celebrity. All this was at no use as at the end of the day, I was left spending sleepless nights and shedding tears on my pillow.

I was now completely into the writing business until the distraction affected my heavy schedule. It was the time when I was dating Gauri; my senior but by the end of our college days she also turned me down because I could not get away from my past. I could not forget Gauri and the time when I had proposed to her, but before she could answer anything I was struck once again with the confusion regarding her presence in my life. So whatever happened to me that day, I decided never to put into a story again, as my life was just fucking me like a whore and nothing else. I concentrated more on my studies for the whole of next year finishing my final year and joined my college hospital internship. I was the first one to be present in the hospital duties every day. I did not go back home even for vacations and applied for hostel. I was allotted the same room in the hostel I earlier had. I was into parties with vehemence; as Gauri also left me in the midst of something like love, just like Priya had done. So parties were a pure distraction and thus were regularly attended.

One day I was in my hostel room when somebody knocked my door suddenly. He was Mausam, my Co internee and friend who had just come from Kolkata for the internship. We had met on the campus a day before and I was ordered by the faculty to take care of him as he was new to this side of the country. It was his second day here at our campus so I invited him for a casual hookup. Being my reader and my fan after reading my book, Muasam was keen to meet me so he took the initiative. He entered my room smoking a cigarette; he put his hand in his pocket to look for another one for me.

"Hi." said Mausam offering me a cigarette.

"Heard of you, wanted to meet you." he continued as I took a cigarette and lit up.

"Thank you." I thanked him for the valuable cancer stick he had just offered me.

"I had read your book: *My Love Never Faked...* and I must say you are fabulous." he smiled.

"Thank you again." I took a deep puff giving room to the nicotine to enter my blood stream for a kick.

"And Priya, are you in contact with her?" questioned Mausam, a query made by millions of my fans.

"No I am not," I tried being straight.

"Oh you are supposed to be together as in the book, if I refer it as your biography," was another expected question and I was tired of answering it.

"It's just a book and books aren't more real than life," I sound exasperated.

"When is your duty?" I tried flipping the topic.

"Next week," answered Mausam.

"With you so I thought I would visit you," he continued.

"Thank you brother for making me comfortable working with you," I replied with relief as I was wondering who my duty colleague might be.

"Have any more candidates joined the hostel as internees?" I threw a query.

"No, not yet, only the two of us" he said in a disappointed manner as he knew about the workload we would have to cope with.

"It's so boring here! Any plans?" I tried problems into finding his preferences.

"Why don't we share a few drinks and have some fun?" Mausam suggested being more frank this time and that's what I wanted from him.

"As you say," I smiled back.

"Then let's have a party tonight only. Let me arrange something for us" I bent down in search my bag. I put my hand inside to look for my favorite liquor stored in it.

"So are you writing anything these days?" asked Mausam as I went to the bathroom to wash the mugs.

"Yes last year I was, but now I am no" I replied.

"Like?" he questioned.

"What kind... another autobiographical love story?" he continued to be curious.

"Yes" I nodded.

"Priya again?" he looked deep into my eyes.

"No, Gauri" I try to maintain the contact.

"Who?" Mausam questioned again.

"My last love. Since then no love and no love story," I distracted myself with placing the mugs on the study table and made a perfect 60ml starter drink.

"What?" he replied astonished, as he could not believe my words.

"Yes my love, true; the one after Priya" I replied and went to the washroom again to get water from the basin to dilute the drink.

While diluting the drinks with water, "I hope you don't mind but we use the water from the basin, its safe."

"Does love happens twice?" he was surprised.

"Yes, it happened and I lost her again" I handed him his drink while I took the first sip of mine to check its *Mixology*.

"Sadly…" Mausam made a weird face after finishing his drink in a single gulp, a hard thing to do with 60 ml, while I took my place next to him with my drink still in my hand.

"What exactly happened?" Mausam looked at me with his eye wide open.

"So you will not stop with this question answer round," I felt annoyed with his continuous questioning.

I could easily find my harsh words had made Mausam feel bad. We remained silent for the next five minutes. We had our next drink and I started answering his questions.

"So you mean love can't happen twice?" I looked into his eyes repeating his question.

"Ya," he answered.

His words and the alcohol took me to the past...

"It was the time when I was over with Priya and Gauri took me out of it with her presence." I start narrating the story of my life a little dramatically.

"She was an awesome girl not just because she looked pretty or she had perfect curves. She was so adorable that everyone fell for her. She was perfect in all ways with a pious heart and a soul of an angel."

"And she was my senior," my eyes were stoned at the wall trying to recollect her face.

"Then what happened to you people? You dated around?"

"Yes everybody knew about us in the college."

"Oh!"

"So with the senior I must say great attempt..." Mausam provoked me with a smile.

"So she is gone now and you miss her?" he probed with his

monotonous tone.

"Yeah she is gone now."

"Why don't you call and tell her that you miss her?" Mausam suggested.

"She is completely gone we have broken up," I gave my final verdict closing this topic.

"But why…" Mausam was not in a disposition to end it unanswered.

"It happened like this: On the convocation day I was supposed to propose to her and maybe she was ready for with answer but I did not propose being confused that I loved someone else."

"Who?"

"Diva; another girl. She was my classmate."

"Gauri stepped away from me and I could not do anything other than repenting"

"Man this is sad you left a loving heart for someone else."

"I know and I left empty handed; it happened itself for which I could not react much."

"But you admit you people dated." Mausam was confused this time.

"Yes I did that but as a friend; this is a feeling no one can understand," I tried my best to confuse Mausam by playing with words.

"All she gave me was a last smile."

"What did she mean?"

"She meant: **Once a loser is always a loser**" I laughed aloud over my destiny.

"And at that time I dated my teacher too," I knew something like this would make him more curious as he was losing interest in my story.

"What a fuck!" came from his mouth and we had a large drink.

"Yes I fucked her," I patted myself.

"Oh God!" Mausam's expressions were frozen.

"Why don't you turn it into a story, process it and serve it hot to your lovely readers?"

"Yes, I tried but then stopped as I reached the bit about the teachers. I was confused whether to write about or not."

"C'mon man this is the best thing I have ever heard. You just put it into words and I can assure you, people will love it." Mausam was excited.

"Really I don't think this thing will sell much."

"Let' see."

"It's late now I think I must leave," Mausam moved towards the door after finishing his drink.

"Okay" I replied back with a handshake and he was gone leaving behind, a thought that something like that could also be put into words.

Next morning

The next day when I woke up, it was already high noon. Being worried and in a state of depression, I put my head on the pillow once again. I then decided to make two small drinks. I was drunk again afterwards. As there was still time for my internship to start, I was in a mood to dope myself hard. I felt twitchy, I decided to consider the suggestion Mausam had given me about working on my manuscript putting my life into a book my next book. I was still not sure whether I would be working on it or not it had been halted long before, so I decided to give a start to it again.

I switched on my computer and started from the last chapter of the book. These were the last memories of incidents that happened between me and Gauri. Just a night back in the conversation, my wounds had been strained. I started typing about my break up from the time when Gauri and I had parted, a very distressing moment for me. Now I was writing my second book and from the last chapter of the previous one. It went as…

LAST YEAR AT MY SENIOR'S CONVOCATION AND LOSING GAURI:

It was one of the most anticipated days of my life. The result was out. I was glad to find myself closer to the ace. I knew the convocation would be a perfect time when I would meet Gauri again. Something fishy was still there on Gauri's side. She was familiar with all my previous sexual escapades, but she respected me like always. Moreover, she was my best friend all these years as we shared so many memories together. I loved this girl; she was awesome, and I never hesitated to tell her anything.

Both of us knew that this was the last time we were going to meet, so I decided to propose to her. I never wanted to propose to her as I was scared that if, she rejects me, it would be an end of my friendship with her as well. However, her charm was irresistible enough to confuse me. For the last few months, she had been talking to me in a caring way that confused me. Maybe I expected some spark to be ignited between us.

Sometimes her jealousy when I stalked other girls would assure me of her feelings. In the last, few days of my college I could not even help her to pack her bags, something I always regretted later. And to my disgust when it was time to be with her, I busied myself with other work ignoring her. She didn't talk much then; maybe my attitude was to blame.

The convocation, this was the only fair chance for me to confess whatever I had in my heart. I decided that I should make use of the prospect.

++*Some wise words: Luck is like fuck the more you have the more you expect.* ++

And to my good luck for the very first time I was called by Gauri for her convocation, or maybe she gave me the last chance to express my feelings for her.

++ *Someone has also wisely said: Fuck love and love will fuck you, they are in inverse proportion to each other* ++

And this is what happened that day. Gauri called me intentionally to give me a chance to prepare to her. She called me up excusing herself for arrangements, which could have been easily arranged by her.

Finally, the convocation day arrived and we were in the hall.

It was noon and the day was hotter than usual, making me tense as well as overwrought. I took a seat next to Gauri. She was sitting with her friends. As I sat next to her, our hands touches each other and we looked at each other puzzled. I didn't know where and when to start. For a moment, I forgot myself sitting in the convocation hall and everything seemed to slow down. I only remembered that it was my last chance to express my feelings to her.

The convocation started. Students were called upon with their name and roll numbers to receive their degrees on the stage. Gauri waited for her turn. While waiting, she repeatedly gave me signals to make a start, but I could not.

I finally mustered courage and started the conversation in a confused manner.

Gauri looked at me and tried to contemplate on what I wanted to say and nodded as an agreement that she understood what I was saying.

"Ever since the day, when I saw you for the first time I had this thing in my mind that one day this beautiful girl will be my friend." said I confidently.

"Hmm" Gauri hummed, along with me and as I played with my words, trying to channelize my conversation into a proposal. I realized it was tough to utter the three words to my favorite senior.

"Are you trying to confuse me?" Come-on you know what, even a mother doesn't feed her child if it doesn't cry for milk, and if you want an answer you need to ask me," said Gauri, as direct hit.

"Yeah" I looked at her again.

"I know this might be wrong as options are open to you, and you might wonder what kind of a person I am," I said all together.

"I feel very easy in front of you; as you heard me; you cared for me and this is something, which makes you adorable," I made a perfect start and a proclamation.

"I was thinking the time spent with you is so memorable, then why not living this life with each other. We can make this life worth spending together," I continued.

"A life-time"

"We are together; we will be in contact," Gauri replied.

"I mean not in the way like we are now" I said.

"Then how?" Gauri questioned.

"Let's be in a relationship... I mean if there is any possibility," I asked her and waited for a reply. I knew I sounded childish for asking such a question.

And I stared at her lips searching for an answer. Gauri stood up. I looked at her.

"What?" I asked again.

Gauri could say nothing immediately.

"My name is announced and I am going on to the stage," said Gauri while making a move to get on to the stage to receive her degree.

"I will give you my answer soon when I will come back," said Gauri smiling.

"I think you can wait that much if you talk about a lifetime..." she continued.

"Yes I can wait for a lifetime. You take your time. I am here only looking at you and waiting for you to come back with this same smile and an answer," I whispered.

I knew from her smile that the signal was clear.

"That smile on her face signals that she needs me; I am blessed with love again. Oh! Forgive me God for what I did to others," I said to myself.

I knew she was the kind of girl who would hold me when I fell. Support me whenever I needed it. Someone, who cared immensely for me without expecting the same, not just because she was my senior, but because she was the most perfect girl around.

As Gauri started moving towards the stage, I kept watching her. I was lost in time. Waiting to hold her and never let go. Time seemed to be frozen. I felt my mobile vibrating in my pocket.

Rings

I glanced at the screen of my mobile. It shook me. I got goose bumps. I could not react to the name on the screen.

Diva was calling me; she was the one I had been dating in the past, but she ditched me for someone, and I was left with only one option in my life- Gauri. Her name was beeping on my screen, which still made me remember the promises I had made to her. I picked up her call with fingers crossed.

"Hello," said Diva from the other side.

"Hello" I greeted.

"Can I talk to you for a while?" said Diva in an apologetic way. I was stunned. I could not react to anything. I was not in contact with her for the last few months. She was busy with Kabir, her new boy friend. I still remember that I gave her my final decision with my last letter. Then why she was calling me, and I was confused that from where she got my new number? I was hurt because in that relationship, I gifted my soul to her, and she sold hers for a relationship with a guy who never cared for her.

I could hear a weep from the other end. Diva was crying, and she tried hard to hide her tears but her agony was obvious. I too could feel the pain she had in her heart this time.

"What Diva?" I asked worried as I still cared for her.

I knew I meant nothing to her now, but I still had same feelings for her. I managed to hide and ask her why she was crying when I knew I had no right to ask her anything.

"I just want to say, you promised it once that wherever I go, whatever I do; you will never forget me and I still have a chance come back" said Diva.

She was behind all those sleepless nights I spent. If I had the chance to roll back, I might have, but I had just proposed to Gauri, and I was in a cheerful mood waiting for Gauri's reply. I did not want such a thing to happen right now to me.

"I could not get you," I said after a pause.

"Can you come out of the hall?" Diva requested a favor.
"Where are you?" I inquired.

It was unbelievable that the girl had traveled all the way from her place to my college just to talk to me. To confess and share the words of love with me, but for me to trust her was thorny. It was tough to believe that she loved me so much and she had come here just for me, but I still could not believe that she was standing outside.

"What do you mean?" I inquired again.

"Yes outside the hall I want to talk to you," said Diva. I disconnected the line and looked at the stage. Gauri was still waiting for her turn to receive her degree and get a photograph taken with the vice chancellor. I could not walk even a single step, but somehow I managed to come out while Gauri kept watching me from the stage.

She expected me to be standing there in the front row when she received her degree. It was a special moment for her, and she wanted me to share it with her.

I came out of the hall searching for Diva. Diva was standing under the sun looking as beautiful as always and my heart skipped a beat as always. I felt that I was meeting her for the first time. I came close to her. Before I could tell her anything or inquire, Diva…

"Let's make a fresh start," Diva said as a tear rolled down her cheek. "You know when I started questioning myself, it didn't take me long to break off because I was cheating on you and myself too." Diva cried out this time. She was all in tears.

Her tears were shining on her cheeks under the sun like pearls. I wanted her to cry for me like I had cried for her. It seemed natural justice.

"I could never find my happiness in someone else, betraying you," Diva continued.

"Now what's that supposed to mean?" said I.

"I never think about it, but I didn't come clean like you. I just told you the story behind the story. You left me... May be it was better for you, but I am fading each day as I am away from you..." Diva confessed her pain to me.

"I want you back," Diva continued.

"You think it's funny?" I questioned.

"No! However, I am now trying to make the best of a bad situation I created."

"I think you are pissed off and trying to get something out of nothing," I replied to tell her that time has gone by since I needed her.

"I know I am left empty handed," babbled Diva.

As I was talking to her, I saw Gauri standing behind her looking at me, she came closer from the other end searching for me.

"Are you guys going along?" she asked, with a smile on her face. It was a fake one as I could notice, but it was very hurting for me; more than Gauri. I knew she might be hurt at that point of time. "I would like to introduce you to...," said I, as I searched for an appropriate justification to introduce Diva.

Before I could say anything, Gauri completed my sentence with "best friend"

"You must be Diva right," said Gauri looking at her.

"Ya" Diva looked at her in a strange way.

"You know what, there was never a day when he had not talked about you, I wished to see you," said Gauri to Diva.

"To see someone who could be so much loved" Gauri added while looking into my eyes.

I broke the eye contact and looked down. It was very painful looking into her eyes.

"No one deserves you better than him" said Gauri with a smile; Diva too smiled at her.

Gauri was helping Diva and me to be reconciled.

"Why don't you shake hands? I don't' think you have as yet. So get along, you need some space," said Gauri going away from us.

"I think I must go" said Diva while moving away from me and then she never looked back. I kept on watching her, but she didn't turn. I wanted to call Gauri back, but I could not as my tongue got paralyzed. I moved the other way while Diva followed me and Gauri walked her own way.

Mobile beeps

Gauri's messaged me on my mobile. I read the message.

It was: 'I know you love her, so never let her go. You have done a lot for her."

While reading the message, I held Diva's hand and looked into her eyes. I hugged her as Gauri's words in the message made me realize me how much I loved her. I had not realized it when I was running away from Diva.

As I hugged her tight, a thought for Gauri came into my mind. I pushed her away. Divas looked into my eyes to search for a reason.

"I thought I was charming?" Diva was confused.

"Yeah baby you are still charming and always close to my heart," I replied.

"But I have to have a talk with Gauri" I continued.

I ran towards the hostel and went into the building; I rushed towards Gauri's room. The room where arrangements for her were made was already locked. She was gone and the thought that I could never meet her now shattered me. I ran towards the car park. I could see her car from a distance, on the ignition and ready to start. I was far away from her car, but I ran towards it, thinking I might reach her before she sped away.

I ran last but could not reach her; I called out Gauri's name loudly. I knew I could not run anymore I got breathless. I could only remember the last eye contact I had with her through the rear-view mirror of the car. I stopped now, but the car kept on moving. I lifted my hand and waved at the car to which she also waved her hand out of the car. The car kept on moving, and finally, she was away from my sight. Both of us could feel the pain at that moment, the pain of a burning heart.

Diva came close to me.

"What happened?" questioned Diva, still confused.

"*That's true Love*" I said pointing.

"*Love, true in nature…. Sacrifice as its cost… one we love need not be along… love should be there always…*"

"*Love is not to keep, not holding; it's to share and owning someone is not that you love a person. It's letting go and as you move out… your presence should be felt with your absence.*"

Diva did not say anything she just kept listening to what I said.

I imagine how many hearts I hurt to get Diva in my life.

I looked at Diva. She was looking down; thinking "**Was she worth it?**"

Typing a perfect end, I switched the laptop off as I felt tired and fell asleep.

That night l concentrated working on my Blog and for a few more days. I let the new book thing go and completely forgot about what I had written for Gauri in my book but to keep my fans updated I just named my new book: *As Long as I Love You,* my second book-coming soon and made a blog post.

{Alcohol doesn't console, it doesn't fill up anyone's Psychological gaps. It never comforts man. On the contrary, it transports him to the supreme regions where he is master of his own destiny}

-Marguerite Duras

CHAPTER 4

As for my periodic check of emails and replies to my fans for various queries over the story one day I received this very special mail from one of my fans subjected: **"HATE YOU FOR PRIYA."**

It was something unexpected these days as now I was enjoying a very successful career in writing and a respectable life vis a vis my readers. I was trying hard to be in a cheerful mood every day. I opened the email and minimized it to load. Then after few hours of writing a few pages of my next book I felt tired, and turned off my computer. This email went into the ashes unnoticed in my mail folder but after 10 days again I received something from Pari, the one who had sent me the earlier e-mail.

After 10 days

As I switched on my laptop and logged into my messenger, suddenly I receive a friend request from an ID: **CUTE_GIRL.** It was an unknown ID but as these days I was receiving regular friend requests, so I decided to accept it.

At the same time, as I added her to my friend list, an offline message popped from this ID.

"You didn't reply to my email anyway; hope you had read it." I tried to figure out what had happened as I claimed to reply to every single email within 72 hours. However, as I dug deep into my mind, I tried to recall the emails I had answered these last few days. Then I opened my Yahoo email, looking for this particular email, but I could not find it. To my last attempt, I opted for a brief search, and finally; I found an email which was marked to be read, but I was ignorant about its content.

Yes, it was from this cute girl who happened to message me on y-messenger. I solved the jigsaw puzzle and concluded that it was the mail I had opened a few days back and left for loading, unintentionally. Without reading it, I had switched off my computer due to which this email was marked as read. Now this email was a source of curiosity for me.

I felt like chatting and explaining my position to her but a moment ago I had deleted her id from my friend list. I felt very bad for her.

Nothing could be done as it was a mail from Gmail, and this girl was sending messages on another messenger.

So now the only way left was the mail to mail apology. Before doing that I decided to read this email to study her mind. I opened and loaded her mail, it was:

So, Mr. Writer

Ooh...You actually did all this to the girl whom you have mentioned in the book? Ellen's tattoo art? And even after reading the book the girl came back to you. What a loser! If I had been in her place would not have. Are you still in contact with each other after the book?? I'm sorry if being a little personal...

However, I really want to know...Because your story seems to be 99% like mine...While reading each page of it, I could clearly recall every incident that happened between me and my guy. One more thing, are you available on the internet or other social media networks?

With care,

PARI

It was like other fan messages, so I opened my folder for the automated pre-written email formats, changed her name and mailed her as a reply. The mail was:

Dear Miss Pari

Thanks for reading and giving me feedback about the novel.

Well, I would still like to appreciate all those who indulged in reading it and making it a lovable one. With all my readers like you, approx. 75,000 copies of the novel have been sold out, and fifth impression is already on the stands and now "*my love never faked...*" is a national best seller. Thanks for reading it.

It gives me immense pleasure when someone enjoys reading my love story. The title of my next novel is: "*As Long as I Love You... I Will Let You Hurt Me*" which is going to be released this year, hope you read it too.

Again, a heartiest thanks. It is my pleasure that you could relate your story to mine and for finding me on the internet and over social media networks.

Regards,

Nikhil Mahajan

Author: my love never faked...

Then I attached a sample chapter of my latest book along with my email to tell her about my work.

Suddenly, someone knocked on the door. I switched off my laptop and opened the door to find Mausam standing outside with a bottle in his hand. "Hey let's drink man." He said as he entered the room.

"Ok." I smiled.

"Hey are you writing something?" Mausam looked excited about what I was writing.

"*Naah*" I try changing the topic.

"Come on you were," Mausam said again as he filled our mugs. "No I was answering one of my readers," I replied while picking up my drink.

"Pari" I continued pointing towards the laptop.

"*Ahan* boy got some fans," as Mausam said as he sipped his drink with a smile on his face.

"Nothing like this" I felt shy.

"This girl hates me on account of Priya" I continued.

"Oh!" I could see a plastic smile on his face.

"It happens," I replied in a very casual manner and yes it was common for me to receive such emails.

"Yeah I know" he also tried to change this topic now, and we concentrated more on our drinks.

As we started with the second round we started having large pegs. "This is my last one I don't feel like getting more drunk."

"Ok" replied Mausam.

"I can't satisfy everyone with my writ ing," I continued with our conversation.

"Hmm" he nodded.

"So, what about the new novel? Did you start writing it?"

"I tried" I could not change the topic nor lie this time.

"Can I read it?" Mausam was curious and put a hand on my laptop not able to resist him.

"Okay." I surrendered to his curiosity.

I opened the file for him; he started reading, and I enjoyed the music as it played on.

After finishing the chapter Mausam exclaimed, "This is awesome!" "But you left Gauri; this is sad," He added.

"It happened itself. I told you *na*. I had finished my drink, so I lay on the bed to comfort myself.

Mausam had also finished his drink, suddenly some mischievous thought hit his mind "Let's do something interesting with this empty bottle."

"Like?" I gazed at him as if I knew he was going to play some idiotic game with it.

"Let's play truth and dare," and as he rotated the bottle it pointed at me after turning 360 degrees. Mausam found a chance to question me.

"What would you choose a truth or a dare?"

"I would say truth rather than dare," I smiled.

"So tell me the truth. Did you try approaching Gauri after what happened?" it was a bitter truth of my life, my past flashed before me like thunder.

"Well Gauri approached me a few months later," I replied with a smile as I put my hand over my head.

"What?" Mausam was surprised this time.

"Don't tell me she did!"

I nodded at his question. I enjoyed Mausam's reaction and I loved his expression. The way his eyes were wide open searching for an answer, I quite enjoyed it.

I started narrating the incident.

After Gauri went missing from my life, I was unable to patch up with Diva.

++*As someone has said wisely," Once a loser is always a loser"* ++ So, I was losing out at each moment when I thought I was winning. Before I could win Diva, I had lost Gauri. And before I realized it, she was gone leaving me with nothing more than repenting and shedding tears.

However, destined for something else just two months after Gauri left me in the midst of a relationship, I received a call from her.

Rings

As I looked for the number, it was a surprise for me to receive a call from Gauri. I could not believe my destiny.

Gauri wished me, as soon as I pick up her call.

"Who's this?" I confirmed.

"Gauri here." she said in a low pitch.

"You even forgot my voice or what?" she continued with a taunt which was very hurting.

"No I left Diva," I said without anything asked.

"Why?" Gauri was disappointed.

"I think I am in love with you" I said without thinking. I was true to my nature and was just taking a risk now without giving a second thought to the consequences.

"I called you up for something else. This thing shouldn't crop up," she tried changing the topic.

"What?" I questioned.

"Come to my place after three days for my sister's engagement," she gave me a telephonic invitation, and I was excited about it. I knew she loved flowers so after three days I traveled to her place with a bouquet. I went to the given address. Her house was all lit up with a merry look. Everyone had left for the occasion except her servant who was staying at her home.

Rings

A *bai* came from inside as everyone was busy attending the engagement and had gone out.

"Where is Gauri?" I asked her.

"Who?" she said with her eyebrow-raise.

"I mean... Where is the engagement?? I try making sense this time and make her understand as she seems to be new or just hired for a few days.

"Ok" she tried to be familiar.

"Go to Mount Hotel" she replied.

I took the same taxi waiting outside to Mount Hotel. As the taxi headed towards my destination, I looked outside with excitement. I kept touching my bouquet for Gauri and a million thoughts raced in my mind. What would I say when I meet her and how would I propose? It was a life-and-death situation.

A tear rolled down my cheek. Mausam looked into my eyes, "What happened next?"

To understand what happened next, you would have to travel back in time with me. I opened my cupboard and looked for a bottle and made a neat attempt to hurt myself. With two such gulps, I continued the narration again.

@ Mount Hotel

Happy! But confused and with a bouquet in my hand I was unaware of the storm heading my way. Life was never as simple as I thought. I had had something store touch in for me.

++ It is wisely said: Things don't turn easy for us; it's just we become stronger to face them and that's what happened with me that day. ++

Everyone was busy enjoying the arrangements that had been made for the marriage except me. Gauri's relatives were everywhere enjoying themselves, but I was busy looking for my girl in the huge crowd of strangers. I tried her number a couple of times, but it was busy. I knew no one was there to help out so it was like solving a puzzle all by me. I kept looking for her.

One of the boys offered me a cold drink. I took one to hide my nervousness. Then again, my search started; finally, I realized that I was looking in the wrong place because close relatives would always be present near the arrangements made for the groom and the bride. I headed for the stage.

As I came close and looked at the bride standing these; I could not believe what I saw. It was Gauri's marriage; I was attending. She was looking lovely as a bride. I could not believe my eyes, I began to tremble. It was very hurtful. I managed to put the cold drink down on the floor and could not believe what I saw. I was too late to tell her that I really loved her. However, nothing could be done now.

Suddenly, as the cameraman asked Gauri to pose, my eyes struck hers and she gave me a smile and an invitation to come on to the stage which I could not refuse. With a heavy heart, I went on to the stage holding the bouquet in my hand awkwardly; I congratulate the couple. There I was, standing as a wedding guest next to the girl I wanted to marry, while her husband stood on the other side.

As I bent to congratulate, Gauri, she said, "Please don't leave without having food and do watch me going to my new house."

For the next couple of hours, I remained there with a heavy heart looking at her, and Gauri kept on staring at me finding me hurt. This was something I never expected, but it just showed how much I had hurt her. And finally as she moved for other ceremonies, I went home shedding tears with the pain of losing someone so dear to my heart.

"That's really hurting, wonder why she did this to you," questioned Mausam with a sad face.

"Hmm" I was numb; I could not reply instantaneously. I cleared my throat.

"This is sad man, I never expected this from her," he said again.
"Nor did I," I replied back.

"But there are things beyond our control and expectations," I continued.

"But I got my answer then" I smiled as I looked at him.
"What answer?" Mausam was confused.

> {When a girl marries, she exchanges the attentions
> of all the other men of her acquaintance
> for the inattention of just one}
> -*Helen Rowland*

I continued

After one month, I was at home shedding tears for Gauri. I tried her number millions of times, but her mobile was switched off. I wanted to know why she did this to me. However, I had no connection with her so it was hard for me to connect. Finally, a day came.

Rings

It was Gauri's call.

"Hello"

"Gauri?" I confirmed.

"Yes" she sounded listless.

"Gauri!" I took her name again.

"Oh I thought you had changed your number" I tried hard over her.

"I don't know I kept this to talk to you," she replied.

"I too did the same."

"Same what?" Gauri could not understand.

"I want an answer from you why you did it to me." I finally asked her, giving a vent to what had been killing me for the last few months.

She finally answered, "You hurt me until the day you left me in the midst of something more than trust. I loved you and wanted you to marry me but that day when you left me, I was all broken from all the places."

"That day I took my revenge"

"I called you up to trick you to attend my marriage; make you realize what you lost."

"I wanted you experiences losing me. I wore the dress we planned together that I would wear at my marriage. Do you remember?"

"That day when you went out to Diva during the convocation, I was planning to make you meet my parents. I fought with them for you, and in the end you left me."

"Sad, Man! This was depressing," I shook myself to reality; my drink was over.

"Why don't you write this too?" he suggested.

{To be ready to fail is to
be prepared for success}

-*José Bergamín*

CHAPTER 5

I comforted myself on my couch and turned on my laptop. I knew that I would receive a few emails from my fans and was ready to answer few of them. It was too early for Pari to reply to me for my automated message. I expected a few hate words from her, and her reply was quite obvious and expected.

She was a bit harsh as always in her messages, and I was apprehensive that someone was playing a dirty prank on me. I was ready for it like always. Her message was:

Hello Mr. Mahajan,

There is still something missing in your story. You call it a love story, but I don't believe what you say. How can someone believe you when you say that you loved someone and you betrayed her the same time expecting an apology from her? This was bad on your part. If I were Priya, I would not have taken you back with your offences. Sincerely, I mean my words. How will you defend yourself to Ellen? She was the one who travelled from America for you. In the end you left her too for Priya. Don't you feel guilty for what you did to Ellen? I think you need to justify it with an answer.

With care,

Pari Sharma

I read the email and replied very politely but this time; I wanted to probe what she had in her mind. For this I knew I had to open up to let her confide in me. So I started retelling, my love life in my email:

Dear Pari,

You tried to probe hard off so today I am sharing my unhappy experiences that I have written in the book *My Love Never Faked*. This was the day when I had my break up, the day I was totally shattered for Priya. The real reason for my breakup was something else. Now you will ask what it was. Seriously, I am unaware of it. I was accused of a crime which I never committed. I was not innocent, but I was not guilty either. I admit I was bad to Priya at times but in a relationship, such things are excused. A relationship is lived in both phases. I was in the worst phase when she left me.

Nikhil Mahajan.

A few days later

As I waited for the next few days and worked hard on my new book, which was tiring and kept me busy, I forgot completely about checking emails from Pari.

Pari also seemed to be busy with her work. One day as I logged into my Facebook account, I received a friend request from a girl named Pari. She was the same girl. I was stunned by Pari's request and noticed regular visits and her interest in my profile. I waited for the right time to add her and then finally she joined my fan club. I never received anything more than a status like from her profile over my updates. A few days later I received another message from Pari as a reply to my previous email. Pari was now introduced to my past, and I knew she would probe me more and more to know it.

Hello Mr.Mahajan,

There is a pain in your heart, and my mom says if you are numb you should share your pain. If you feel free to tell me you can share your pain with me. I hope I am not disturbing you much but seriously if I can not be a part of your solution, I refuse to be a part of the problem. Who knows I might help you in some way. Do reply. I will be waiting.

With care,

Pari Sharma

{ In this bright future you can't forget your past}

- Bob Marley

A few years earlier in my life

Before I was a writer, I was a full time lover. It was the time I was doing nothing in my life, that is, nothing more interesting than loving my girlfriend. I never knew a storm was just brewing as one day I came to know that my girl was going around with someone in her college. I was at home and she was in Delhi. She was out of sight, and it was easy for her to double cross me and I was unaware of the fact. It was her classmate, with whom she was interested and going. I tried to ignore this fact though many of my friends called me up to tell me, but I never believed them. I ignored her for a while and she got the chance to throw me out of her life. For the last time, I went to Delhi to meet her and make a final effort towards a patch up. I was uninformed about the fact that she was ready for the break-up and I was the one who was the sufferer. I could not imagine her in someone else's arms, not even in dreams, but I still tried to forgive everything and I made a last-ditch attempt towards this. I went to her place looking for her all the way and called her up to meet me for the last time.

She had already made up her mind to break off with me.

-@-

1stMarch- Longest Night of my Life

It was the rainy season, and the weather was not in my favor. I was facing rejections and feared that there would be a breakup. My relationship with Priya had been time for the last three years but suddenly her attitude towards me changed. A few common friends believed she was involved with her classmate, but I believed in myself and my love for Priya. Even so, Priya's statements were rather hurting. Her perspective had also changed, and it was high time that I had to make a bold move.

I was in my hostel when it started to rain. I knew Priya loved the rains and decided to take bold step.

Before leaving my place I messaged Priya that I was about to visit her but she did not reply, I messaged her:

"Listen to me please, talk to me, or I'll do something crazy."

I was absolutely shattered. I rang Priya's younger sister. Her number was also busy and I swore. I got so hyper that I threw my phone at the wall. It broke into pieces in front of me. I was extremely depressed by the act. Still thinking, Priya might connect me. I fixed the phone as best as I could and put it on the table. I lay on my bed wondering what I did in my life to be punished like this. Priya always used to tell me that she would leave me, and then I would regret, but I did not expect it so soon. I was about to have a nervous breakdown.

Ringing

Someone called me. Priya's name came first to my mind. As, I looked at the mobile screen, it was Priya's sister who was calling me.

"Hi *bhaiya*, did you call me?" Priya's sister asked, unaware of our fight.

"Ya but you were busy on the phone at that time," I replied back.

"Ya I was talking to *didi*; she didn't attend her college today as she was feeling low, and she felt like talking to me. I find her a bit sad." said Priya's younger sister.

That was it. It was enough for me to take a bold step.

"Ok will talk to you later" I ended the call.

I dialed Vicky, my friend.

"Man I am going to Delhi; I need some money, don't ask anything; just help me out," I requested Vicky.

"When are you going?" Vicky replied, unaware of the situation I was going through. He was ready to help me without any questions.

"Ok the money will be in your account in an hour," he said.

I took out my jacket to protect myself from the rain and a bag with a few important things to help me on the way.

As I took the first step outside my house, a second thought came into my mind. "I should try Priya's number once, before I start for Delhi."

However, my morale was high and I had already decided to proceed; so nothing could stop me now.

I walked to the bus stop, looked for the bus to Delhi. A million thoughts came into my mind.

I slipped my hand into my pocket, took my mobile out to message Priya. It was soaked in the rain now.

"I am coming to Delhi, meet me please. I want to meet you?" and in no time it went into the sent items in my Inbox.

I waited for the reply. Nothing...

The bus arrived; I got into it and took a window seat near the driver, and began my journey.

Priya's thoughts were haunting me. I was in deep agony, and the good weather could not lift my mood. The only thing I hoped to hear was her voice for the last time. I wanted to talk to her. I tried her number once again, but she didn't take my call. I knew she was not at college and was ignoring me. I felt humiliated that my girl was ignoring me. I really wanted to tell her something. I typed another message again:

"I am in the bus, started my journey I'll be there at Delhi after four hours."

She didn't answer.

I tried calling her again; I was terrified at the thought that Priya had finally made up her mind and had started ignoring me but for what reason I did not know. I accepted I was wrong not to call her all these days due to some reason, but my conscience had shown me something else. I wailed a second before something wrong happened. I really needed a chance to resolve it. I tried her number again after it; I started calling her every minute.

Beep

Finally, my phone beeped and Priya's message flashed on the screen:

"I am getting irritated, please stop this."

Finally, whatever these messages were; Priya was replying to me at least. That was enough for me. I messaged her again.

"I am on the way, hope to meet you; I don't know much about the places and your address."

Nothing came from the other side. I kept calling her, but the difference was now that she was putting down my calls at least she was reading my messages.

As it was raining heavily outside; the bus was moving slowly and then it halted for a while at the stop. I was very hungry, so I took a cup of coffee before the bus started on the second part of the journey. I could barely notice Priya's message on my mobile.

"Please don't come I won't meet you, go back home."

I knew she might be with her new boyfriend, but I wanted her to look into my eyes and say, **"this is the end"** and a breakup with a smiling note but not a lie. However, nothing could have been done in these two hours; as most of the journey was covered, and only two-hour journey was pending. And I knew nothing about my next step.

All this was tough I didn't know her new address, and I knew nothing about Delhi, nor where she stayed. I had decided to go to Delhi, and the rest was up to God where he would take me. I was at his mercy.

I knew I was in a problematic situation. I had no money. My mobile was all wet like my eyes with tears. The storm was not just outside; it was totally shaken up within. I knew if Priya didn't guide me, I would have to sleep on the street, but I was sure that I would not go back without meeting her.

I tried to call her; this time to my shock Priya's mobile was switched off. This was the craziest part of the journey. An hour's journey was left, and I was about to reach Delhi so it wasn't predictable.

I called her once again to check her out; it was switched off still. I was clueless. I knew only one person could help me here and that was Priya's sister.

I called Priya's sister again.

Rings

"I am in Delhi and Priya's number is switched off, tell me what I can do now?" I asked Priya's sister.

"*Bhaiya* I don't know much about it, but I can give you her roommate's number; she might help you out"; replied Priya's sister. It was enough for me.

"Message me the number. I don't have any pen to write," I continue and put the line down.

Priya's sister got the hint that there must have been a big fight that's why I was in Delhi to meet her.

In no time, a message beeped with her roommate's name and number. The journey was about to end soon I had to take some action. I decided to call her friend. However, my hands stopped as it was my last hope, and I wanted to keep this chance.

Finally, I reached Delhi. The bus stopped at the I.S.B.T terminal in Delhi. I didn't know where to go. Something had to be done from this point itself. I tried Priya's number repeatedly. This time I was lucky, as Priya's mobile was switched on. It rang but still no reply. It seemed like Priya was really reluctant to take my calls now. I knew she was irked with me. I believed where love exists nothing else matters.

In a flash without, taking time, I typed a message to Priya "I am in Delhi; tell me where to go from here now."

A message came as a reply, "Better go to your friend's place or go back."

It was hurtful, as if she had thrown a stone at my face. It hurt me deeply but my morals were high, so I decided to make my way. I remembered that Priya lived somewhere close to her old home, and that was near Vasant Vihar. So Vasant Vihar was my first destination in search of her. However, for that I had to take bus or an auto rickshaw. I knew nothing about travelling in the capital. I had never been to Delhi. So for me Delhi was a pure concrete jungle and I was lost. I crossed the road and went to the other side of the road. It was raining cats and dogs. I was all wet, but my morals were high. Now I had to take a bus to my destination. I asked a Papad-wala for directions. It was my bad luck that for my G.F's place I had to ask strangers, a place where someone who knew me for the last few years was reluctant to help me, it was depressing. From that very day, I learned that I like walking in the rain because no one would ever know my eyes were wet with tears with my heart thinking; my G.F didn't help, and I had to take help from a stranger.

"Take bus number 621from the other side *Babuji*," said the *papadwala* as I asked him for directions. I crossed the road again. I felt lonely, and I could easily hear each rain drop sinking the road.

I took the bus and started my journey. I knew I had to be brave enough as I would be consoled and encouraged by no one at an unfamiliar destination. I had to move ahead to get the destination – Priya. Travelling in the bus I followed a stranger's advice. Perhaps I would have been lost here in this big plastic city, or maybe I would reach somewhere else, but I had to meet Priya, and that was final.

"Where do you want to go?" asked the bus conductor sitting next to me as I took my seat, next to the door.

"Vasant Vihar" I said like I knew the place. I didn't want him to know that I didn't know much about Delhi.

"20 rupees?" conductor asked for the money. Handing him 20 rupees, I wanted to know how long it would take to reach there, but my heart didn't allow me to ask this. All the passengers were silent. Everyone was enjoying the rain except me.

It was summer rain but for me, it was like my heart was crying. An hour passed by. I was watching the whole scene. Even the conductor didn't tell me that I had arrived at my stop. Finally, I broke the silence I inquired about the stranger near me," Sir. I want to go to Vasant Vihar is it close by?"

"You are there my dear you asked at the right time, which lane?" The passenger sitting next to me said.

A few minutes later I stood up and said "Sector A."

"You are in B-sector better get off as soon as possible."

I knew I was making just a statement and I had to reach that's it.

Now the destination was near but where to go. Finally after getting out of the bus I slid my hand to reach the phone and decided to call Priya's friend.

Rings

"Hello," wished Priya's friend.

"Hi" I replied back.

"Who is calling?" Priya's friend asked.

"You don't know me?" I skipped the introductory part.

"I am Priya's boyfriend; she might have talked about me sometime," I continued and tried to flip the conversation to the important part.

"Yes I remember you; Priya was upset because of you."

"I am in Delhi," I said.

"Why?" she asked.

"I want to meet Priya can you help me please?"

"I can't help you much. Why did you travel so much?" she replied, telling me indirectly that she couldn't help me.

"I travelled for Priya; I can't stand the pain I want to meet her."

"Sorry where are you?"

"I am at Vasant Vihar, and I know, you people live here."

"Yes but we don't live exactly there. It is a bit far away."

"My love can't stop me. Tell Priya to meet me, I am here until dark. Maybe, she can make up her mind, or you persuade her to meet me once."

"I can't help you" she disconnected.

I walked alone at Vasant Vihar. It was unfamiliar; I was now at the PVR Priya market. I saw a board directing to Vasant Vihar. I knew nothing about the place all I know was; I could go to Priya that's it. I was missing Priya more and more. There were times we would meet each other there, but now time turned; she didn't even want to see me and left me all alone in a big metro city. However, things were true; my deliverance made me realize and go through all me things. I decided that whatever it takes I would convince Priya that I really loved her, and I wanted her back in my life, whatever it might cost. I took small strides and finally; I reached PVR Priya, but I knew no what to do next.

I went inside alone. I was missing Priya; it was raining again, and I was all wet, but I could not show my tears as we all know boys don't cry but who's going to notice that I am crying. I needed to cry and so I did.

Beeps

A message popped up. It was from Priya's friend.

"She would meet you in half an hour at PVR Priya."

I typed back "I am already at PVR Priya."

No message came then.

One thing was final that Priya was going to meet me, but it was difficult what to explain to her. I was sad and had no words that could ever repair this relationship.

I was broken by Priya's words; maybe my true love might get me near her. Nothing else could help, I knew well. Waiting for Priya, was the toughest job over, I was starved for her. Yes, I was just dying to hold her hand and tell her to punish me in anyway but not like this, I decided to ask her to slap me, scold me or do whatever she liked but be with me. I kept waiting for hours; I could not even message her. I knew I was wrong, so I had to wait till my life look me to her. Till then, I would wait. I would stay up all night but would not go. Being deceived, I stayed. I kept waiting near the gate, sometimes I went inside; my legs were aching, and I felt that blood was draining from my legs, but this couldn't stop me from meeting her. From here I couldn't move back. Finally, I saw my angel entering with her friend. She could not make an eye contact with me and kept herself as busy as she could with her phone and the caller. She was guilty and to be protective she was with her roommate. I knew she was wrong, but I was here to make things right but the way she came, inside I knew in my heart that it would not work and nothing good was going to happen. Still I decided to try to make things better. I shook hands with her, but my body was numb I could barely say anything at that time. Her moves were decided, and she started walking I could hardly move to her side. I kept following her.

+++ *Someone has said wisely: Any relation would be in a bad phase when two people who used to walk together, were walking away from each other.* +++

I kept following her, and then it struck in my mind; I should hug her and cry in front of her and ask for forgetting so that she gave me a last chance to mend everything. I could make her feel love again and remind her about our beautiful relationship. But my hands were so heavy at that time; I could hardly move. Priya took me into the coffee shop where I had presented her anklets a few months back. She ruined everything, Priya was gone and so was my trust, my relationship, everything. She protected herself by her harsh words that I was wrong in her view and thus I was facing all this but truth was something different. Neither, of us wanted this situation to open up turn nasty. As we went into the coffee shop, it was empty, but we went upstairs. Maybe Priya had to confess something to me. I kept following her silently. Finally, she took the same seat where we had sat the last time. I took the seat facing her. Both of us were silent. Priya wasn't even looking at me. What to do in such as a case? I was like, melting on my seat. Where to start, it was like my tongue was buried in snow, I could not even feel it, how talk.

"What would you like to order sir?" said the waiter. Finally, the silence broke.

"Lemon's tea for two" I ordered.

"No I don't want anything." Priya made her statement before the waiter could place our order.

"Ok sir means one lemon tea?"

"No I said two," I said with a heavy voice.

Priya didn't say anything this time, but I knew she was not going to have it.

"I'll have two," I said to end this melodrama.

Priya was still angry with me, it was clear from her face.

"I told you clearly about the breakup, then why did you travel here?" said Priya in a harsh voice. This hurt me most because I wanted to forget everything that had happened but Priya was not willing to change her mind and now it was clear from her words that this was the end.

"Your drink sir," the boy placed the drinks on the table.

I wanted to tell her what I knew about her and what she was doing to me. However, someone has wisely said that if you want to console the fight, just give it an end, and I was prepared to give a try; if Priya was ready to confront that she was nurturing a relationship behind my back. I believed that if you want to have a break up, don't do it like a coward else there would be only one choice –better be mine again and accept all the mistakes.

"Don't you feel bad for us and for what you did to this relationship when it was going so smoothly?" I said.

"There is nothing left between us," she said harshly.

I knew she came along with her friend as her support. She was standing near the door. I had nothing to say no, so I kept mum.

"Sorry" she could only say this much.

"So finally it's a breakup?" I gave her a last chance.

"Yes." this yes just kept buzzing in my ears, and I felt I would collapse at any moment. I added more lemon to my drink, I knew it would be bad for my stomach, but I gulped it down. My eyes were burning after the drink. I offered her the drink, but she refused.

"Break up" her words made me uptight. I looked into her eyes, this time. I could not find any love for me. Maybe, she had started hating me too and this was something I could not swallow. I took the other glass of lemon tea and gulped it down. Priya knew that I was hurting myself, but she didn't care. Things were changed between us.

"Let's go. There's nothing left for us to debate, you shouldn't have come over here because things don't always work as you plan. Sometimes things happens different way," said Priya ending this date.

The receipt came in a moment, and I paid it off while Priya kept on looking out of the windowpane. It was hurting me each second. I wanted things to settle down but how can I do it all alone. This time I could not hold back my tears. Priya moved out; I wiped my tears and pretended like nothing bad happened between us. I followed her again until we reach the gate; her friend was busy on the phone.

I knew she was calling Priya's new boyfriend, to tell her that things had gone the right way and at present the girl was his only. The past relationship was over. She was now away from me forever. She didn't care to look back.

It was not like she had gone, but she had broken this relationship; I was left alone. I could not take it.

"You go now," suggested Priya as she knew I had no place to go and to hide my embarrassment.

"You know I never go before you; you go and then I will follow."

She took an auto-rickshaw and went off leaving me all alone. I could not do anything. I stared at the road, and the auto-rickshaw got tinier as it went away from me, and finally, I could not see it anymore. I started walking alone on the road I had no place to go now; I could call my friend and tell him that I was in Delhi, telling him to come and take me but there was something else waiting for me. And it again rained so heavily that my tears got wiped away with the raindrops. The clothes I was wearing got all wet and my mobile too; finally ruining all the connections to contact anyone. I sat near the road thinking about my place in her life. With my head in my hands, I looked at the sky.

"I will never come back…" came from my mouth as I stood up and the truth of a silent breakup remained buried in my heart.

As I came back to my senses, I was still wasting time at the road side killing my rescue time. I wished this life to end here right at that very moment. I went to a nearby shop, bought a cigarette and had a puff to relax. "I will keep on loving you Priya," was the last statement I had in my mind. I would not lose her like this I thought. I reached to the last puff of the cigarette.

What happened then nobody knew. That was the longest night of my life, and it really changed me. I started evaluating myself. I looked at myself and at the sky, it was weeping like me but all I could find here were my lapse.

I moved a little more and went a little distance from where I left my past. I reached a bonfire which was prepared by the beggars. As my eyes fell on them, one of them invited me to join. I came close to the fire. I was shivering and wet. For my girl, I was all safe and sleeping in my friend's apartment, but in reality I was now sitting with a troop of beggars. I sat there for sometime with these beggars until it started to rain heavily and then, as I bent my knees to take a stance, one of the beggars uttered something.

"Are they washed away?" said one o f the beggar looking into my eyes as if he knew what has happened to me.

"All but some are still cuffed inside my heart and it pains," I replied.

"I know I might not be rich, but I am rich in finding people," said the other beggar.

"You know why this happened to you?" he said smiling.

"Why?" I wanted an answer now.

"You are made to do something different today," he smiled.

"Like?" I was confused to his statement.

"Wait here with us," said one of the beggars as he pointed to a space next to me.

One of the beggars said something in Arabic, I could not understand it, but it enlightened me. His voice was husky and his words were bold. I just read his pain in his lips and they were enough for me. He again took a piece of paper and read it aloud.

Then one of them lit chillum and offered it to me. I had no issues and no choice, so I took it and had one puff. It was cold, the hot Chillum came to me twice in the round share, and then I felt something good in myself as everything seemed to blur. I found my entire life in front of my eyes. I asked for a pen and paper.

One of the beggars put his hand inside the pocket of his trousers and gave me a diary with a pen. I took them and started writing my life and my story as everyone seemed busy with the chillum. I kept crying and wrote my life on this diary until my eyes shut.

Suddenly, I felt someone kicking me; it was my friend Asif. He wanted to make sure it was me. And with one more kick, I wake up. I found myself sleeping on the foot path on the road side. All the beggars were gone. I was stoned and I had the papers in my hand, but the pen was gone. I got up and realized that I too looked like a beggar.

"What are you doing here man?" inquired Asif.

"I was here." I could only say.

"Get up you idiot and come to my apartment," he ordered.

I was enlightened as I looked at the paper, and knew what I had to do now. As I stood up I saw my friend standing to rescue me. It was the first time I was laughing at this world. I finally realized that those beggars were God's message to me.

I went to Asif's place and stayed there for next few days. His place was near to mosque, and it was Ramzan. I never expected so much from Asif. He took care of me and I too kept the Rozas with him in his apartment. Every evening I would break my Roza with him, and we had food together. The connection to Allah helped me further in writing the next phase, and the corrections were made eventually.

"What do you keep on writing on these sheets?" he asked one day.

"This is my life, my love story."

"And what are you going to do with it?"

"I will get it published."

"You know you found me that day among beggars. Because of this beggar; I got a pen and a paper on which I wrote the story of my life. I am still writing for the right end of the story," I smiled at Asif.

And suddenly with the message popped on my screen, I came back to my present life. It sent a shiver through me and then in the next few hours as I wrote everything in my email and in one click, this email was sent to Pari. I didn't know why I was sending account of my personal life to her, but I was sure that I didn't want to lose my reputation as a swindler in front of her eye.

{When people are true friends,
even shared water tastes sweet}

- Unknown author'

CHAPTER 6

Six months of internship, I was done with the studies with my degree in my hand; I hugged and promised Mausam not to disappoint him and write about Gauri, as soon as I get time, back home. I was now writing the book and was about to finish it. A few days later, as I shared my personal life with Pari, I didn't know why, but I felt there was something. I received an email as a reply to my email from her:

Dear Nikhil,

Thanks for replying me and giving me the real side other than what is there in the fiction. Otherwise I would have blamed you for ditching Priya, but I am still confused about Ellen? I hope you are not fooling me with your words Mr. Writer, I trust you because of your earlier statements that I am the lucky one, the one with whom you shared the truth. I trust you.

Again, good luck to you to write this new book, and I hope this book will be an excellent experience like the previous one.

With Love and Care,

Pari Sharma

With her emails started getting regular, Pari and I got closer to each other. While logging into my Facebook account, I could now see a lot of notes from Pari over my pics and status, quite often from her side.

I was now used to it, until the day came when Pari and I met over Facebook chat for the first time where I could see her message popping over my screen waiting for a reply from my side. I never used to log in over Facebook chat as I could not reply to each and every chat message from my fans; so it was just an initial occasion for me. However, Pari was approaching me in a regular way, and her name was firmly etched in my memory.

"Hi," came from Pari's side.

"Hi" I typed back.

"What's up?' She typed her second question in no time.

"What's new?" she continued.

"Nothing much, all same." I replied back.

"And are you busy these days?" she questioned.

"I was busy with my new book."

"Can you tell me the title of the new book?"

"Sorry it is little secret. I am close to the releasing date. When I sign the contract for it, I will let you know." I replied to change the topic of the new book.

"Well your first book was awesome. I think I had talked lot over it and had irritated you a lot too."

"No."

"It's okay."

"Thank you." and she changed the topic.

This was the first time we were chatting with each other and it was quite confusing what to ask and how to reply, but one thing was sure. It never seemed that we were chatting for the first time. It seemed like we had known each other for years.

"I am still waiting for the reply to my e-mail about Ellen from your side. Do you still think doing such a thing to a girl just for lust? Is it right?" she questioned as she probed my personal life more.

Then she ended the topic with "Whatever you do, better think over what you have done to Ellen. I think she should not have accepted you; as for Ellen you were still doing what Priya was doing with her new boyfriend."

"Hey *chillax*," I struggled to change the topic now.

"This is chill for you think. Is this Ok?" she yelled with her words as she left the chat.

The chat was getting on my nerves, but as she was one of my good fans, it was my duty to hat with her in a normal way.

I was left with no words; I typed "Ok" and "bye" before I left the chat.

Days passed and finally I decided to reply to her. This fan of mine was really close to me now and knew a few aspects of my life that nobody knew. I logged on to the internet with my laptop and replied to her last e-mail inquiring about Ellen.

Dear Pari,

There is nothing to thank about my reply as every reader is special to me and I am a writer only because I am connected to my readers. The part of life you have peeled was almost unknown to anyone, and I don't know why you are so much interested to know more. Still I am telling everything to you.

Last time you threw your anger at me regarding Ellen. This is the ace thing in my book as in the beginning, it was written that the story was fiction, and all characters are imaginary. Ellen's part mentioned in the book has been based on imagination. It was used to pep up the love story. As I always say I am not as great as other people and just a simple person like everyone around. So to evoke curiosity, I just added some juicy bits to my story. This was the reason I used Ellen. Hope you will not feel bad after receiving my email.

With Love and Care,

Nikhil Mahajan

It was the first time I was using love and care for her and telling the truth about Ellen too. I never cleared this with anyone else. Why I was clearing it Pari was unanswerable even to me. She was like one of my favorite readers. I was connecting more and more to her as I answered her emails on the daily basis.

A few days later I received an email from her:

Dear Nikhil,

I am sorry I was harsh on you that day over the chat, and I am really regretful. I think now I had completely understood you but left with one question only and I hope I will get the true answer. I want to know, why you reflect yourself to be bad if you are not, and why you are covering this girl when you know she ditched you? Still you are showing yourself wrong about this world and putting a right tag over her. May I know the reason behind it? Are you still in love with her? Thanks for replying to me for every single email and giving me the real story of your life else I would have a false image in my mind regarding you. I would like to share my part from you that I was given this novel by my boyfriend as an example that how a person can be incorrect like you and be forgiven for the mistakes; no matter what they are if you truly love them. Isn't this shit? Tell me, do you agree or disagree? And are these meetings in your book real? Please do send me something more from your next book as I am very keen to read it and any news from the editor for its publication as to when we all fans are going to read it.

With Love and Care,

Pari Sharma

As I read her email, I mailed her a answer a few hours later.

Dear Pari,

You yourself have answered your question. You know what is there in my love story. Whatever happened whatever I lost; love won in the end. That's what I wanted to show. Where there is love, there is nothing else, nothing like guilt, jealousy and breakups. And after you gel with your boyfriend I am glad about my purpose of writing books is fulfilled as I believe if I am able to save a single relationship I am done. Yes, these meetings with Priya are real incidents. So I am keen on your favorite incident from the book. Let me know which one it is.

Well, from my new book I am sending you a blurb along with the email. Please find the same.

With Love and Care,

Nikhil Mahajan

As I enclosed the blurb of my forthcoming book along with the email titled As *Long as I Love You*, which got published a few months after and turned out to be a best seller. The Blurb I attached was:

BLURB: NOT LIKE ANOTHER LOVE STORY

A stolen story manipulated and published...

A friend to answer

Manav in love with Diva confuses himself to Meha....

Dah! A love triangle

Kabir, Diva's boyfriend... Shit happens.

Karan a true spy friend and the rescuer...

Gauri, Manav's senior and his crush....

A teacher... and a mysterious friendship

breakup and make-ups.... A state of confusion

Hostel parties.... Friends and a bet

The story orbits around Manav...

The Protagonist and various situations...

"LOVE HURTS AS LONG AS YOU LET IT HURT YOU"

And then...

After this nothing happened further and no reply came from her again, so she got long forgotten. I got busy for my new book and its cover design.

{In her first passion woman loves her lover,
In all the others, all she loves is love}

-ShareGeorge Gordon Noel Byron

CHAPTER 7

This was the first time I was writing the truth to someone as the real me and what exactly happened in the life; in the past rather than what I hid in my book.

Dear Nikhil,

I think we are turning out to be friends, are we? Do you still consider me only as your reader? I read your new book's blurb, and it seems to be pretty interesting but only one thing I could not follow is the teacher part and the mysterious friendship whereas in your previous book I love the Anklet incident, and it's my favorite one. It's so lovable; hats off man you did something in public for your girl.

Great and I hope you keep on doing such extreme things in your life. Best of luck with your girl and live a good life. Take care of her always.

Thanks for always replying to me I know I am on to your patience but...

With Love and Care,

Pari Sharma

As I read the email and the Incident about the Anklet, Pari's favorite part of my life took me to the past; a few years back when I traveled to Delhi for Priya to gift her anklets; I had just bought for her. I was not familiar with Delhi and Priya was my GPS system for the route. Travelling for an hour in the interiors of the capital I finally reached Priya's market may be 15 minutes late or so. However, rather than being happy for me, Priya's face was cherry red, and she was a bit upset. I jumped out of the rickshaw with a big smile on my face and flowers in my hand so that she wouldn't have any words to say. Looking at the flowers the redness of her face just faded in a second. Priya really loved flowers; I knew it. All her anger vanished, and we started to walk while I looked into her eyes. She was so happy to see me.

"You rascal; why didn't you tell me about your visit?" Priya screamed angrily.

"Hey I tried to call you a couple of times," I answered in a witty manner.

"You would blame me that I don't pick calls, and then you say to look; I came from so far for you, and you didn't take my call," yelled Priya, but it was in a loving way as her anger vanished with my smile. "I don't need alibis; ok let's move from here and go to some good place, where we are all by ourselves," I said.

"Now let's have coffee," ordered Priya.

"Ok" I replied with a smile.

Then we started moving towards the coffee shop. While we were moving our hands were touching. It was a soothing feeling; with a second touch or two, as I put my little finger into hers, suddenly a bond of love got shared. I held her hand it was a magical moment... I received the same reaction from Priya's side too; she also held my hands at the same time, and we went into the coffee shop holding hands.

Entering the coffee shop was so romantic. Lights were dim with sweet music playing, just the way I wanted at this time. We went up stairs so that we could talk.

As we reached the first floor, it was full of love birds. As we know *Delhi is dillwalo ki.* While sitting I was still in a confused condition when and how to make the move. I had those anklets in my hands, now all I had to do was to them to give her, but crazy thoughts kept buzzing in my mind. It was decided by me that I'll not present anklets to her, but rather I'll bend down and tie them myself. However, the thought that everyone will notice this act was damping. I could not gain much courage. Priya kept watching me and found that something was there that I was hiding and she could feel my discomfort.

"What are you hiding?" Priya asked me with a smile on her face, as if she knew I had something for her.

"Nothing" I replied.

"Don't hide" asked Priya.

"Well there's something Priya but this isn't the right place," said I.

"If the thing is special, then the place is right too, so I want to see it now," she commanded.

"Ok" I said while bending down, but I could not reach her ankles. "You can sit with me," said Priya.

I went to the other side of the table and sat beside her.

It was not easy but I didn't have a choice, because I had already done it thrice without succeeding.

"Can you sit with your leg crossed?" I asked.

"Ok," said Priya sitting the way I asked her to.

The very moment she did; I tied the anklet on her ankle with a smile on my face.

"That's for you honey," said I.

"Now how about the second one?" I asked. Priya could not say anything, the scene was so emotional that she kept staring at me, and I could find the aura feeling for me.

That was awesome the way I wanted to be. All I wanted here was to hear those three pious words – *I love you.* I kept watching her lips if they move a bit for uttering the golden words.

I could read her lips saying "Love you" to me.

It continued until the coffee came, and the eye contact broke. Priya was feeling so shy she could hardly look at me while she was busy stirring her coffee. An hour passed, and we couldn't talk about anything. We had our coffee further being silent. Then it was time to depart; I felt heartbroken and didn't want to leave, but had to. After payment of the bill, we moved out but this was different the way we moved inside the cafe. I moved ahead, and Priya followed me. We both were shy. While moving out of the market, finally it was time to depart, and I had to take an auto rickshaw.

"Wait a minute," Finally Priya said something.

She wanted to say something. I was expecting something like- "Please don't go or love you."

"Where is the other anklet?" inquired Priya.

It was still with me right there in my pocket.

"The other anklet?" she repeated.

"You lost it somewhere," I said.

"This is not done; you don't care for my things!" I exclaimed. "No really…" Priya was in tears; she was afraid not to lose it at any cost.

"Let's see there at other places together" I suggested.

I knew the anklet was there in my pocket. I continue the mischief; I went inside again to the coffee shop with Priya.

"So where did you lose it?" I asked.

"I don't remember" said Priya with a soft voice in a guilty manner. Moving to the other side of the market, it was a pretty lonely place and there was a fountain.

"Sit here and let me check where it is," I said in a bossy way. Priya sat on the bench saying nothing. I bent down bringing out the other anklet from my pocket and secured it on her ankle. Priya was still unaware of what I was up to.

"What are you doing?" Priya was still tense.

"So here is your anklet darling," I said surprising her.

Priya looked at me with a big smile as if she had found some treasure. I laughed at her while Priya was in tears.

"You cheated me and now you are laughing," Priya shouted at me.

You cheated me…

As I memorized her face with the word cheat, I came back to the present, and a current ran through my body. I felt guilty of loving her. I went into the bathroom. I took my razor blade and slashed my forearm with it as many times as I could so that I could bleed. I went into the shower and remained under it. The blood kept dripping down my forearm hurting me. There was something more hurting, and it was the incident about the anklets, which hurt me further. This was a part of the story, unknown to everyone. A few months earlier before I went to Delhi to gift the anklets; I looked for my purse to see if I had money, and unfortunately, they were empty. I called Vicky and Asif to help me, but we were all students so it was difficult for them to help me to give such an expensive present. So my other buddy Varun suggested to me to work part time.

"What kind of work can I do Varun?" I asked him.

"Tuition," Varun shouted his magic word with open arms.

"What??" I inquired again as I had never thought of such a thing. However, I had no choice so Varun took me to a place where these fellows used to inquire about home tuition. As we entered the office of Home Tuition, I was told to wait for a short interview, and in two minutes, they called me.

"What are your qualifications?" questioned the boss.

"I am a science student,"

"Ok, I have two inquiries; one for Math tuition and another for science you can go and teach which ever of them suits you," I was given two options now.

"How much will I be paid for it?" I inquired.

"Rs. 1500" he replied back.

"But I need Rs. 3600"

"I don't think we can afford to pay so much for a science teacher," he replied.

"Only if you were a math tutor, we would have paid you Rs. 2000," he continued.

I could not think much as saying yes for math tuition, but it was hard for me to teach someone a math's equation. I had no options and no way out. I came out of the office with a smile. Varun was waiting for me outside.

"So what did you select?"

"I said yes for math."

"You are going to teach math?" Varun was surprised.

"Not yet but I will learn to."

"C'mon, there is nothing in this word that cannot be done for love," I stroked his back as we went out of the office together.

And then, I tortured Vicky for the next two months to learn math from him. With all the patience I could muster, I went to a house to teach math, a subject almost unknown to a science student like me. Adding a good sum to my account; finally, I managed to gift anklets to Priya.

As I turned off the shower, the blood still dripping from my forearm, I grieved for doing so much for a girl who betrayed me in the end. Everyone knew about what I did for her but nobody was aware how I did it. Pari's question again scratched my wounds.

As I typed the whole incident on my laptop, I mailed it to Pari as she liked this incident, and she deserved to know what was happening behind the scene.

{You're the most beautiful woman I've ever painted.
Not because you're beautiful but because I'm in love with you.
Hopelessly in love with you}

- *ShareMuriel Box*

CHAPTER 8

No reply came for a few weeks, and I got busy with my new book. I was writing something about a teacher-student relationship, a confused love. I wrote few controversial lines for my next book without thinking of the consequences:

She was my instructor on whom I always had a deep crush, one of the gorgeous women of the college and was what every man's desire. Whenever she used to come to the college with her close-fitting jeans, she would expose her thighs and her perfect upper curves. I was one of the students; who love imagining and extremely fond of her, watching her in the class all the way attending by sitting in the front row just for her, and it was something I was doing from the very first day of college. She was the most radiant and delightful woman on the campus.

One day in the library while I was searching for a book, I saw a lady who was little senior to me standing near the book shelf searching for a specific book; wearing glasses. Her attire was like that of an angel. She was wearing a white tee and blue pants. Her shirt was not sizable enough in measure and was just giving a kiss to the upper border of her pants. While she could raise her hand to reach the book, I got a good glance of her beautiful navel. Her navel ring was rather seductive. I wanted to see more of this girl. I kept looking at her and thought of putting my hand across her waist and fondling her navel but suddenly the books from the rack moved, making space for this girl to look on the other side. She came to know that someone was enjoying her beauty. And when I saw her, she was my teacher, my angel Miss. Sehgal. Oh God! She was really looking like a college girl. Short, sexy and in my dictionary, I could not praise her with any words. However, her expression said, "Idiot! You are looking at your teacher" I felt embarrassed this time. I looked back into my book, and it was the end of a beautiful mirage. She went off taking the book, and I don't know why I followed her to the desk. She went into the teacher's section for reading her book, and I took a seat just behind her so that I could see her. She was engaged in her book while I kept looking at her. I was unaware that she was looking at me in the mirror while I was gazing at her and searched for the color of her panty, which was clearly visible. She stood up and came to me at once. I look at my watch as the library was about to close, and I was relaxed about the fact that she might be leaving but her steps advanced to my table. I felt panic stricken. She adjusted herself next to me and with a little fishy smile, she looked at me.

"What were you looking at?" questioned Miss Sehgal with a harsh look.

"Nothing," I answered and shivered.

Her fen, her body aura was awesome and soothing.

"Well you must be looking at something or searching something... in this book, else why you are sitting here in the library for so long?" said Miss. Sehgal.

I took a deep breath as the question changed which she asked first, and it was something answerable.

"Well looking for some conceptual reading here and some of the words are tough for me; I wonder why it is the part of our syllabus?" I said.

Oops, these were unintentionally some wrong lines from my side and hurting for a teacher.

"Well for a student like you who looks into the things without understanding the fact," the words were again alarming.

"I never liked this subject," I went straight to my point and hide myself and my inner consciousness of peeping at her.

"Well do you have a bike here?" she came close and whispers while standing up.

"Yeah I do," I replied.

"Well come along with me to my flat, and I'll give you a simple book, take it along and drop me home too," she said with a little bitchy smile on her face.

My new book had stopped at this point. What to write about the association between a teacher and a student and up to which limit was a big question. Whether they should go physical or just end this with a slap. Attempting such a relation was tough and uneasy without an association.

My pen glued to a level where I was keen about Miss. Sehgal, my teacher and had fantasies about her. However, should I go further than that was a big question? As I completed writing a single chapter of my book, I was undecided about this chapter, whether my reader would accept it, or consider it shit.

I rested for a few hours, and then I decided to delete it. With a click, this story went into the bin and the concept of a new book was also deleted. I was unhappy as I could not write anything now. Indian culture might not accept such a story. I stopped my story here and took a break for the next few hours.

As I had nothing to do I just kept busy with few emails and then suddenly I found an email in my Inbox, and it was from Pari:

Dear Nikhil,

It made me weep to find what you did for your girl, but I am delighted that you people are together after so much. However, I want to tell you here that such a thing has happened with me and my boyfriend. But I never intend to go back to him because for me once a betrayal, there is always a chance of betrayed no matter from which side.

Your part regarding the teacher is still pending and I am keen hoping as a friend you will share a few more pages from your next project with me. I assure you that it will remain confidential as our little secretive friendship.

I am desperately waiting for your reply regarding the part about the teacher.

With Love and Care,

Pari Sharma

I knew after reading my email, she had started feeling good for me, but she still didn't know that I was not fixed with Priya again ever and still in a bad shape. However, who cared! These were my personal concerns and need not share them.

Dear Pari,

I don't know much about new-age thinking, but I want a little help from you; I hope I can get a true answer as to what new age thinks about a teacher student relationship, their love, which turned into a physical relationship. I know this is a very touchy subject, but I wish to write about it. I need help and suggestion.

With Love and Care,

Nikhil Mahajan

Her reply came in the next few hours:

Dear Nikhil,

I don't know about what you are writing about. This relationship is hard for me to defend, but I know one thing. Don't worry; whatever you write people will welcome it if you write from the core of your heart. Trust yourself and do take suggestions from Priya too she will be a great help.

With Love and Care,

Pari

It was a confident and short email from one of my readers who eventually turned out to be my favorite. Before the email, I was not sure about the level of relationship to pen it down but Pari showed a keen interest in that part so it boosted me up to take it to the next height. I started my laptop and undeleted the chapter where I had ended up with the teacher in her flat and started scripting:

I wrote few pages where the two came close and then I fitted the encounter where the two went physical. Now I was sure that I could turn this relationship into an idyllic matter so that readers would enjoy the lusty encounter. After being into bed for several times with her and finally, on the day as we apart finally, I pen down the lustiest incident to it' core as:

As she opened the door, I could find the mood changing. Sehgal was looking as seductive as she could. I had never seen her look so sensual. Her room freshener was my favorite jasmine. The room was clear. Candles were lit and were placed near the bed, windows and on the table. A perfect ambience as we say. I looked at her as she opened the door; she was wearing white shorts with a transparent tee. As I entered the house, Sehgal closed the door, and we could not resist hugging like we were starved of each other.

"Hardcore, I want it this way," said Sehgal with lust in her eyes hugging me tight. I gaped at her. I could not understand her words. "I know what you want and searching in me for the last few days and I am ready to give what you want," Sehgal said looking into my eyes passionately.

"I want you to love me with your lust, which is visible in your eyes, and I want to see how much you can," she continued. She knew this was the last time, and she wanted it to be memorable. I came close. She was different from every girl I had met. I knew she was not my love. I just lusted for her. I was approaching her knowing we were doing it, just as we were fulfilling each other's need in every way. As I slid my hand from behind into her tees, I was all prepared for the move, but she was a little more practical than I could imagine. Her command over sex was more than I had and so I was just a student in front of her.

"Come closer and I will take you to heaven," she said like she possessed me and I could sense her passion.

"How?" I asked inquiringly and desperate to know.

"Shut up! You are not supposed to ask me," as she threw me hard on the bed.

I kept tight-lipped, being frantic, could not control myself. Sex was not new to me but the way she was going about it, was different and I didn't know how not to behave like a little' virgin in front of her. However, thanks to my first interaction with an experienced lady who was introducing me to this world. I followed her command. As she unbuttoned my shirt I just lay there with my arms open looking at her, into her eyes as she moved her lips over my chest and kissed me everywhere. I could see the sexual desire in her eyes. I was helpless in front of her beauty. Her dominance challenged my manhood; I got hold of her hair firmly and made her come on top of me entirely. As her lips hit mine, I kissed her hard to gratify my thirst for her. She also kissed me on my lips, and they were ultimate to suck. I held her hard over me, and she just relished me. I tried to unbutton her shorts.

"Wait a minute," she ran towards the kitchen with her unbuttoned knickers and half worn tee and her hair untied, brushing her body. It was an erotic sight.

I raised my head to view what she was up to now. She came running with chocolate ice cream in her hand and threw it on my chest. "I want to lick it all," she said as she put that cold chocolate ice cream over me.

She put some of it into my mouth, and I sucked it hard, and then she sucked the same finger. I was like a little sex toy for her; I sucked her lips as I wanted to taste her part of the chocolate which was the sweetest thing I could ever get.

She licked the rest of the chocolate ice cream spilt over me and teased me until I begged for more. She unbuttoned my pants as I opened her shirt along with her bra and threw her nude body over mine. The chocolate cream was now on us both, and we started licking the ice cream on each other. I slid two fingers inside her vagina and try to find her G- spot. I knew it well if I had to satisfy her today; I had to make her cum once before I go inside her. With art of oral and then 69, finally we went for a proper sex in missionary position; later crashed on each other with over juices secreted all over. Lying beside her naked body with her in my arms and looking at the ceiling and thinking what we were doing a minute ago.

"You want a cigarette?" said Miss. Sehgal to me as she lit one for herself.

"I'll have from this yours," I replied pointing at the cigarette in her hand.

After two puffs, Sehgal handed me her lighted cigarette as she searched for the ashtray.

I took a puff and as Sehgal slid herself over me to reach the ashtray kept on my side table. I kissed her body in response to which; Sehgal kissed my lips.

"Thanks for this time," said Sehgal handing me the ashtray. "You should not be, I learnt a lot from you," I replied back.

"One thing..." said Sehgal to me as she clicked a pic of me with her mobile, sliding her head close to me to be in the frame.

"For the memories we share," she uttered.

"And whatever happened between us, it is very memorable for me so please let us end it all, as there's no future. So we will maintain a professional relationship forever," she said in a way, which was quite persuasive.

I held her hand in my hand as always, and she put her head over my chest; kissed me again leaving me on the bed alone went to the bathroom. She was naked, and my eyes followed her as she moved around to change. Her butt was amazingly raised and was impressive maintained. As she reached for the door of the bathroom to enter she looked back and caught me gazing at her naked body.

Back into my book, I ended this chapter with courage that I could put such a thing in my book, I was eager to share it with Pari. So I sent it to her with my email to get her suggestions and reactions. This was something Priya used to suggest me most of the times, but she was not with me now.

A few days later I decided not to lie anymore, and finally; I mail to Pari about my status to be single.

This is how it happened one day in the chat:

Pari: "So how's your work going on?"

I: "Great I am about to finish"

Pari: "And the teacher part, is it true?"

I: "No common do you think I am doing it?"

I: "L.O.L. I was just joking."

"Hehe…" she typed.

Pari: "So what about Priya?"

Pari: "How is she now?"

"She is fine and doing well on her own."

This thing shook her up "Well on her own… what do you mean

Mr. Writer?"

I: "I mean I am single, and most of the people don't know"

"But why?"

"Didn't she come back? However, in your story, you wrote something like you, and Priya gelled together."

I: "That was the story. This is the truth."

I: "Ellen is a story and Priya didn't come back."

Pari: "Are you hiding something? Is there is any Priya or not?"

And with her words popping on the screen it took me back to my worst nightmare of my life when I had seen my girl in someone's arms. I came to know about her relationship, and I went to the scene where the two lovebirds were dating. I hated myself what I saw that day after I had broken up with Priya for no reason.

{**For it would be better to die once and for all than to suffer pain for all one's life**}
-*Aeschylus*

@
—14 Feb—

Finding a reason for no to me from Priya, finally, the day came and I was there in her city to see everything with my eyes. I took a bunch of roses for the girl and dressed up as I used to meet her. I went to the place where they had both decided to meet. I entered the hotel. It was near her PG accommodation. I took a seat from where I could see the whole space but remained hidden myself. I ordered a soda and waited for the lovebirds.

Unaware of my presence, Priya and Kabir entered the restaurant in a very intimate fashion. Kabir's hand was on Priya's waist. They looked very intimate. I could not hold the sight, but it was the truth at the end of the day; I had to face. I react very normally keeping a stone upon my heart and stabilized my outburst of emotion. I try tried to see what they were up to. They took their seats. Priya was wearing something flaunting her beauty to get an appreciation from her ex. Her top was short and rather revealing; I could see how everyone in the restaurant looked at her. I always knew Kabir was a stud, and Priya could do anything to impress him as he was the first love of her life. It was not easy for Priya to forget him. I had tried my best to overcome Kabir but now the results were in front of my eyes. Kabir asked the waiter to take the order and while placing the order both held hands and look into each other's eyes. Kabir was saying something to Priya and she kept smiling at his compliments with a blush and a smile. I could feel how happy they were together. Where did I stand in her life? I could see Kabir's toe rubbing against Priya's thigh.

I could not see any more so I tried not to look that side. My heart was numb and I could not react. I wanted to go and slap her just there in front of everyone, but I knew for the past few months I had been playing with fire. My hands had to get burnt. I was left empty handed now so I did not owe her anything. I did not believe anyone when I was told that the two of them met at times like the time when Priya had gone for a tour and I was watching the entire thing there. I was helpless, so I decided not to give a last try and to go back home empty handed. It was hurting, and I did not want to face Priya because my trust was broken.

I went back without saying anything. Before leaving the place I tried to take a last look at her. I saw what I never wanted to. The two kissed each other and as their lips touched, a tear rolled down my eyes. I knew I was not going to meet her, but I wanted her to know that I was present at every phase of her life. I called the waiter while the two were happily enjoying their date. I gave a note written on a tissue paper to him and a tip of 100 bucks to give her. I switched off my mobile and went out of the restaurant crying hard. I wonder why every time I was a shipwreck, there was rain, but I thanked God it rained so heavily that day and my tears got wiped away with those raindrops. The clothes I was wearing got all wet but the cigarette still lit with two puffs taken from it, it also left me like my girl sat near the road thinking about my value in her life; for hours as with my head on my hands I looked at the sky.

"I will never come back... I got my answer" came from my mouth as I stood up and this time I went towards my friend's apartment and the truth silently remained buried in my heart.

With a tear on my cheeks, I came back to reality with so many messages from Pari's side:

Pari: "Hey you there?"

"Say something"

And dozens of such messages while I was all soaked in the memories. Finally, I typed everything and emailed it to Pari as what exactly had happened to me.

I lit my cigarette and taste a deep puff while looking at the screen for the next 5 minutes and in anger, I banged my head against the wall in despair. I kept myself busy then for the next few days with a trekking camp to overcome depression.

After a few days passed to my email, she replied with just a single line: **"TRY TO PUT IT IN YOUR BOOK BECAUSE THIS IS THE TRUTH"** and a temporary phone number as she was not allowed to keep one.

After few days I felt like wishing the cute gal, so I message her "Good morning"

"Who's this?" A text came from the other side.

I messaged back "It's me Nikhil."

As soon as I opened the delivery reports suddenly my mobile rang.

It was a call from Pari.

I picked up the call.

"Hello." I wished slowly.

"Hi" shouted the girl aloud with excitement.

I could feel the happiness on her side to talk to me, but I kept myself a little low.

"How are you?" I asked as a regular conversation.

"Tell me first how you like my voice?" she asked.

"It's nice… I mean sweet," I replied.

"I know everyone say am melodious." and then suddenly she said someone might be her friend spread the ward around that I was calling and everyone almost started screaming my name aloud. I felt weird and with a little quarrel among them, the call got disconnected. I put my mobile aside and smiled over the incident. My phone rang again from the same number.

"Hello" whispered Pari from the other end.

"Ya," I replied back.

"My friends want to talk to you…I just ran from there," before she could continue someone pleaded with her to which she handed her mobile to someone else.

"Hi, I am Payal" that was a husky voiced girl.

"Hi Payal"

"I am a great fan of yours and so is my friend…" Then suddenly Pari took her mobile back.

"My friends are excited to hear you, sorry *haan.*" said Pari.

"I didn't know you were my fan," I replied.

"I will call you after some time," she tried to skip away from her friends who were intruding on her privacy.

"Bye" and the conversations' ends.

A message came then and there, "If you are not busy, I will call you tonight."

"Not at all and free tonight," I texted her.

A few hours later at night Pari called me up.

Rings

"You know I am very excited talking to you, you are my favorite author," said Pari.

I just laughed.

"Why are you laughing?" said Pari.

"Because you are so kiddish," I replied.

"Hey don't call me kid."

"Really?" I taunt her.

"Yeah just because I have no boyfriend doesn't mean I am a kid," said Pari confessing more this time.

"So what it means is that if you had a boyfriend you were not a kid," I said taunting again.

"No not exactly, just told you I am single but you can flirt" said the girl flirting with me.

"Really?" I replied back in the same tone to make it a game.

"I was trying hard with you. I just felt bad as I came to know you are engaged," said Pari to me.

"Awww!" I replied back.

And we talked over flirting for the next half an hour.

"So Priya will call you anytime and if she comes to know you are talking to someone at this hour you will be in trouble."

"No," I replied.

"Hmmm. Trust right," Pari made a self-statement here.

"No" my answer remained the same.

"Then?" Pari was confused by my monotonous tone.

"Because Priya is not here, she never came back."

"What?" Pari was totally confused now.

"Don't try to have fun with me Mr. flirty writer," she continues thinking I was playing a prank on her.

"Really I mean what I said. I don't have anyone now, I am single... Priya is gone and it's been a long time."

"You are joking?" Pari found it difficult to believe.

"If I was Priya I would have came back," she said disappointed and her voice seems to turn sad with each word.

"Yea I know but..." I stop in the midst of my sentence with a deep breath.

"Yes I am not Priya and that's the reason you are saying so and fooling me," Pari took it again as a prank from my side.

Before I could justify my side and tell her the truth, due to some signal problem the line just got very noisy and then the call dropped down. I did not try to call her and neither did she.

Next morning a text came early morning: "Is it true that Priya is not with you?"

"Yes" I texted back.

"Oh how sad."

"Why are you sad for me? You should not be sad."

"No, I am sad for Priya"

Then another text came from the other side: "I am also single."

"And now you are trying hard on me," I texted her back.

And for the next one week we just talked endlessly over the mobile. We both started calling each other on regular basis turning her favorite reader and my friend.

{If you say, I love you, and then you have already
fallen in love with language, which is
already a form of break up and infidelity}

-Jean Baudrillard

CHAPTER 9

One morning over the chat, Pari decided to share her cam with
me. I was too excited for it as it was the first time I was going
to see her. Her Facebook account even had some fake picture. So I
made up my mind easily for sharing webcams.

Soon I received a cam request from her.

"So we are going to share webcam" Pari typed excited.

"Yes" I answered hiding my thrill.

"You first Mr. Writer," she made a one-sided option for me.

Since I had no choice and wished to see her, so I started.

"Now it's your turn?" I messaged her back.

As I accept the request for her webcam, her messenger webcam popped over, and now I could see her on webcam. However, there was some problem. Rather than showing me her face. I could see her hands typing and something like potato chips which she was eating that time.

"So miss. Your hands are beautiful but the cam is not just properly adjusted," I typed back to her.

"LOL" she replied to me from her id.

"What make you think about this id- Cute girl?" I questioned her.

"Because I am," she replied back.

And then she tossed one chip from the table and had it. Suddenly, something struck her mind and she offers me one wafer from the webcam.

"You want to have?" the girl was senseless, but I was relishing the experience.

"Thank you" I typed back.

I had nothing to talk about now. Neither could I see her face. I changed the subject and did not ask her again so that I could not show her my excitement.

"Which one are these and which is your favorite wafer?" I asked her one of those idiotic questions.

She texted: "Uncle Chips" and tossed one wafer again.

"Uncle" I ask again conforming.

"Yes Uncle Chips," said the girl again.

"Aunty Chip's *nahi*…" I prank this time.

"LOL" and type passed so quickly with her.

Time always passed so fast with her, I could not believe. I never felt much relieved after chatting with her. She was not a part of my routine. I like enjoying myself with her.

And then one day I was offline I received an email from her saying:

Dear Nikhil,

I am going so don't call me. My dad will be here. Keep yourself busy with your books for a few days. I will be back soon. I need to study too for which I need time and space.

With Love and Care,

Pari.

I didn't call her for next month and kept myself busy with the book. Finally, the day came I got my other book published. I was so happy to share this news with Pari, but her number was switched off. I decided to put a mail to her account so that she could be a part of my happiness.

Dear Pari,

I hope you are studying hard and doing fine? I got my book

published, and I would love to send you a free copy of it as my first reader. Hope you have time to reply to me. Waiting…

Regards,

Nikhil Mahajan

I was feeling disturbed without any contact with her. She was my daily routine, and she was absent. I was now over with my work too, which was keeping me busy. I had nothing to do and her memories were haunting me.

To keep myself occupied I decided to travel all over India promoting my book. This thing engaged me for a few more days. I tried to meet people promoting my work, it was a thought that I should meet and it was a good chance, but Pari's mail shook me up.

Dear Writer,

I am deleting my account, but before I do something like this, I would like to tell you that these days when I was with you were the best days of my life, and I could not resist loving you. You must be feeling weird that someone you were talking to like a fan is in love, but I think I fell in love with you. I don't know if I ever connect to you, or maybe it's a bye note for the last time. Falling in love with you was easy but to be with you is hard as you might be receiving such notes from many girls. Where do I stand with you? I know I am just another friend for you, but I hope I remain special forever.

Bye once for all,

Pari

I kept thinking that Pari might be infatuated and talking too much made her conclude that she loves me. I kept my work in priority and went to the book fest at Jaipur. I searched my mobile and checked my Inbox for mails. I could not believe myself for such a quick reply with a subject BYE FOREVER from Pari's side. I felt restless. As I opened the mail, and read it, I felt fidgety. I decided to move to Kota to find Pari. Before leaving for Kota, I tried Pari's number of several times so that I could meet her, but it was switched off. I felt there was something wrong. I mailed her, but I didn't seem to be connected with her, and a Demon mail came back saying that there was no such email address. It seemed like she deleted her email id. I felt more and more restless. Then I finally open her Facebook account, which was deactivated. I opened my Mail account to check her email id correctly, and I found nothing. I felt like I was in love with her and had some connection with her.

{With reason one can travel the world over;
Without it is hard to move an inch}

-Unknown author

CHAPTER 10

I packed my bag, and was ready for an endless journey. I knew it would be very tough, but it was not new to me. I was now going for Pari and not Priya. However, what's the difference; the two situations were not different. I had no address, but I planned to head for Kota without thinking what to do.

The next day I started my journey from Jaipur at 10 o'clock.

I knew nothing of this place and had no place to go; it was my last option now I knew no one I looked around. I had no option other than calling for help. I opened my bag it had nothing good in it to help me out.

I traveled without any information; it was not worth it to travel for two more days. I found my way to Allen's Institute for help, but they were not willing to provide information about a student. Finally; I decided on a very old trick; I started throwing a tantrum over them to which they agreed to give me just her home address. She was from Kangra, Himachal Pradesh. I was now destined to travel across Kangra from here.

The Second part of the Journey

I started with my journey. I was not feeling well. I knew something bad was going to happen. I was pretty sure it would not be safe. My first stop was Delhi, which seemed to be almost impossible without tickets.

I went to the ticket window.

"When is the next train to Delhi?"

"After three hours."

I looked at my watch; I was not sure if I could reach Delhi on time from Jaipur station.

"One ticket Please"

"Okay"

With the ticket in my hand, I was ready for my journey. It was a local ticket class 3. I went to the platform. I stood there for next two hours.

"When is it coming?" I asked a guy standing next to me.

"Don't know" he replied.

I stood there for one more hour, but this train was late as it seemed. It didn't come for the next two hours. Suddenly, as the train arrived on the platform. I knew I would not be able to get a place to sit as a lot of people happened to travel with me. I stood at one door looking outside. It was a miserable sight. We were so tightly packed. I was afraid of pick pockets. I put my purse and money in my front pocket. The journey took six hours and I was absolutely exhausted. I traveled for the next six hours standing. My legs ached a lot as I reached the Delhi station.

As I saw the train for Jammu Junction, I ran as fast as I could. The train was about to start and as I reach the platform, it started to move. I ran along with it, and I hopped into the nearest compartment. I sat there on the door until it stopped and I searched for my seat. For the next six hours, I traveled without any ticket. I knew the ticket checker would come and check me for the ticket, but I had no time.

I board the train to Pathankot for the next part of my journey.

Pathankot to Himachal

I had thought chasing my life and love would not be a tough job.

However, destiny had something else in store for me. Before my eyes could cry the clouds cried as much as they could. I was in the bus on the way to Kangra but due to a heavy storm, the bus stopped on the way. I was confused. I looked at my watch; I was getting nervous with every drop that poured on the road making it more dejected for me. Even so, this was a tough journey, but it was the journey of my life, my love; I asked the driver if there was any way out.

"I can't help," he told me.

"Why?" I asked.

"Look at the road."

I saw that one side of the mountain had just fallen over the road. The landslide had made the heavy rocks fall on the road and it was a dreadful sight.

"Can I get something if I walk to the other sides?" I inquired.

"I can't say."

"Can I try?" I asked one of my co- travelers.

"It's dangerous," he said.

Faith on God, I put my first step on the clay soil, and it just sucked my foot 1 foot deep. I was scared, but I still gave it a try. I held on to one of the fallen tree branches for support and I tried to pick my foot out of the mud. With one hard push I was out. It was at the edge of the mountain. My hold got tighter this time. I held my breath as I saw one stone rolling down the mountain with a push from my foot and it vanished as I looked for it. I was scared. With very light pressure, I traveled for the rest of the route and in a minute with some courage I was on the other side of the road. It was still raining heavily. I waited for the next half an hour until I got one of the taxis. It was ready to travel back as everybody knew this landslide would not be cleared up till morning.

It was late when I reached Kangra. The last stage of my journey was over; now I had to find Pari.

The next morning I went to the given address in search of her home. I knew I would trouble her if I made a hurried entry. So I waited for her on the other side of the road near her house. I kept waiting for the next three hours, suddenly I saw a girl coming out of the house on a scooty. I shouted waving my hand, but she could not hear me. I was left helpless on the road. I ran for an auto rickshaw.

"Where?" the driver asked for directions.

"Follow that scooty," it was already out of the sight.

"I will pay you double," I pointed out the direction the scooty had taken.

As the auto rickshaw traveled to the other block of the street, I could finally see her Scooty parked outside a restaurant. I went inside.

She was with a guy; I could not believe that I traveled so much for a girl but my bad luck never failed to travel along with me. The way they were treating each other, it seemed as if they were in a relationship. I tried not to interfere but being courageous and heart broken this time; I went near her to ask for an explanation. The guy was just about to kiss her girl.

On her lips a tender kiss

A love note with a smearing throat

I will say "love you" once again

A chocolate bar in my hand

A bunch of flowers along with it

Waiting for you on a very summer noon

Travelling all the way

In a place I never stayed

Still going with a hope

That I will never betray

Today making it as special

Going on a date surprisingly

Waiting for her on her way

A little far where she stays

What I saw I could not believe

My girl in the arms of someone else

Could not believe them they so close

Passion taking over the stars

Making her feel special as I tarnish

Sadly! On her lips a tender kiss

But by someone else as I miss her lips

My feet stuck in their place, but I was decided not to move back without talking.

"Pari!" I murmured as I reach neared the two loving couples.

"Yes?" both looked astonished.

"This is Nikhil here," I tried introducing myself.

"Yes what can we do for you?" both looked uninterested.

"Do you remember me?"

"No"

"Hey man you are trying to steal my girlfriend in front of me."
"No"

"I mean she mailed, me that's why I am here."

"Aren't you from Allen Institute?" I asked.

"Don't you remember me, Nikhil Mahjan; writer" I tried to explain.

"Nope."

"Who the hell are you, excuse me?"

"The book: my love never faked; you mailed me, we talked and chatted over the phone, do you have a Facebook account; you are Pari right."

"You have mistaken me for someone else may be."

"Sorry" I try to move out now.

As I took a few steps, I thought to confirm again.

"Hey." as soon as I could say anything her boyfriend punch me on my face and I fell on the chairs. My lips bled from the blow I just received. I could not stand.

"Let me say something."

"Shut up you are trying tracks on my girlfriend in front of me. You think I will stay here listening quietly to you?" her boyfriend blew on me.

"Bastard"

I try to recover myself, and as I stood again.

"I am the writer who wrote *My Love Never Faked.* Do you remember me?" I said everything in a single breath.

But her boyfriend was not in a good mood to listen to my silly things. He gave me mother blow on my stomach this time putting me down in trouble. I could not breathe properly, and I lay on the ground; he kicked me once again in my ribs with anger.

"Do you get me?" he shouted.

"Okay bro," I said huffing with a raised hand; telling him to stop.

"Stop it," shouted the girl holding her boyfriend's hand and there were tears in her eyes. She was scared.

"You move out," said her boyfriend throwing her on the other side.

"I need a help if it's not you, then it is someone from your friends who might be using your ID," I again asked.

"No" girl stood there crying helplessly.

I took a seat nearby placing my hand on my stomach to hold the blow, and it's after effect.

"Hey I remember a girl who used to read a novel with a big flower on it a lot. She was so fond of it." the girl tried to remember something.

"It was some love story," she continued.

"Yea that's the book I am talking about," I smiled. Blood was still dripping from my lips. I spat on the other end of the table to throw out the blood to enter my food pipe.

"Who was she?" I then inquired.

"I don't know her exactly."

"Still any clue?" I looked into her eyes.

"She was from the both medical stream and medical stream, but I was in engineering, I think she got admission in Delhi University." she said whatever she knew.

"Thank you" I thanked the girl for the information, and started to move out. However, there was something I still needed to do. I looked back and in a fraction of a second I gave a blow to her boyfriend on his face. He fell down.

"Respect the girl," I took a fighting stance.

However, her boyfriend was already down.

"Thank you but you should have asked me before putting a hand on me," I said and I went to my hotel room to pick my up bag for the final lap of my journey.

From Kangra to Delhi.

Now I knew D.U. was where I was destined to go. And I knew before going back to my place I had to halt at Delhi.

{We must love one another or die}

-W.H. Auden

CHAPTER 11

Finally, after a long journey all across the country I was in the capital. I reached DU, the sight was awesome; I trembled as I took my first step. It was huge and too big for me to look for this particular girl whose name and identity were still unknown. All I knew about her was that she studied and did her coaching from Allen's Institute, Kota. Whom to ask and where to go was a very big question for me now. I started moving inside the University; I felt just as if I was there for Priya. What I was confident about was I would get this girl because my morale was never shaken in her search.

Now it was a hard time for me as I moved inside and asked the gate keeper as he looked for my identity and my University card.

"What do you want mister; I think you are not from this University so you better show us your Identity else be out"; I was brutally questioned by the gatekeeper. The way he inquired seemed like he was used to such trespassers. Now my entry was tough.

"I am new here and I am looking for a girl whose name is Pari." I replied back.

"Which department?" he questioned.

"That I don't know, but I have to find out," I replied.

"I mean is she a non-medical student?" he inquired.

"Hello, trespassers here are strictly prohibited so better fuck off, or else I will call the police. You know what kind of charge will be leveled against you?" he looked pissed off this time at my idiotic answer.

"It may ruin your career too," he continued and tried to scare me. "I am being polite to you sir, please let me in. I am really in search of a girl here who I know from Kota, and she is a student here now."

"But I think you cannot get her here" he looked bossy.

"Why?" I questioned him.

"Because it's a huge University with 52 departments so better call her. He gave me a last chance to try and call her so that I could meet her." His move was decided.

"You are bluffing I think. So go back where you came from," he kept discouraging me.

"That is the problem sir I don't have her number," I again gave a lame answer.

"Are you up to stalk some girl? You are a crazy fellow!" he shouted angrily this time and looked away. He did not want to talk to me anymore.

With his harsh words, he pushed me aside. I felt very bad but being courageous I move again and went in front of him. With both my hands folded, I pleaded for entry.

"I am sorry boy you are wrong; this trick will not work here," He whistled for more security and in a minute, I was thrown down on the road. Helplessly, I dusted my trousers and look at the gate. I knew I could not get across the huge walls of this university. It was like wall of China.

This was my first attempt to make a foolish entry into one of the colleges in the Delhi University and from here as I looked at the other part of the road I could see few more colleges. I had to try to search her. It seemed to be an impossible task now. This University was different from rest in the country. Then suddenly, I saw a banner about the fresher's party in the evening. This was the only chance for me because I knew she had got admission recently, so this was a good chance for me to look for her but to get an entry here was a hard task.

I moved out and went to a nearby shop and ask for a cigarette to think of some way to get in, I lit up my cigarette.

"Has anyone even tried to enter this University, without permission?" I asked the paan-wala.

"*Nahi bhaiji* but it was once said that a few guys entered from the back gate when I was a kid," The paan-waala replied.

"This was at the back, right?" I pointed towards the other way. "Yes there is a little jungle. There you have to be good at climbing or else you will fall and will break your bones," he tried alarming me. I went back and walked for about one km into the jungle, I still found the wall to be very high. I stopped there looking at a tree nearby or any place which I might not have noticed or help me climbing. However, I could not find any, suddenly...

"You want to make an entry?" asked paan-waala as he came close to me from one side.

"You are still here?" I was a little surprised.

"Ya just came to see how you will climb it up? It's not at all safe," he smiled.

"Yes I know"; I replied.

"Then?" he asked me as if to investigate my mind.

"I don't know how but I only know I have to" I answered making a move to get a support from the wall.

"Let me help you," he picked up a spade in his hand and hit the wall with it.

"We will break it," he showed his intentions and his hand for help.

"We will break it for you and..." he gave me a smile while I took hold of another spade and hit the wall hard.

For the next two hours, we struck the wall with the spade to make a perfect cavity for me to get an entry. And with a step I made an entry; I found a wave of fresh wind touching my hair. I felt blessed with luck and a smile and sweat on my face I felt like I had won this world for my love while the Paan-waala remained there smiling and satisfied.

"Now you will get that girl," said the paan-waala to me.

"How do you know that?" I questioned him.

"A few years back I made an attempt to enter the University for my Girl." he looked into my eyes.

"Then did you get her?" I asked in curiosity.

"My girl was gone but all I got was a punishment," he said disappointed.

"I was suspended from my degree taken into custody; my father left me, and then I never studied," he confessed.

"Will tell your story next time you meet me here…,"

I hugged him hard and stepped side. It was too tough to try a University for finding a girl without any name and description. I made a move and went to the hall, and there I asked a student, pleaded him to help me for which he was ready to help me at last. And after a few hours, the party started.

FORM AAKHYAA'S PEN:

From here I, Aakhyaa want to narrate what happened. I was very busy with my life as I was new to the college. With my last email to my favorite writer Nikhil, I moved out of his life completely but one thing I never told him that I had started loving him so much that forgetting him completely was difficult. Gradually, I came to know how pure his heart was. However, for an ordinary girl loving someone who was an accomplished writer was very common but for my favorite writer to love me was a rare case.

But destiny had something else for me, and that day changed my life. It was the fresher's party, and I was all prepared for it. I was in my best dress that day; I don't know why I looked so beautiful as if I was getting dressed up for Nikhil. I was little nervous but ready for my fresher's party. I went into the hall. Cold-drinks were served, before the curtains could ascend. Suddenly, one of my seniors came on to the stage and made announcements on the mike.

He announced: **"I have a special message for someone here"** everyone gazed at each other.

He continued: **"There is someone who traveled across all for a girl whose name he doesn't know but for a true heart and love for someone he is here"**

Then he put his hand in his pocket to search the message slip, read the name and announced it aloud: **"Pari where ever you are and**

listening to this message please go and meet Nikhil on the terrace."
"He is waiting for you." and it was me with the tricked name Pari;
I just felt like collapsing while everybody clapped and hooted aloud.

"How can he find me and be here?" I asked myself and started
shivering.

"This is Nikhil, my favorite author, and he is here for me." I
smiled with tears in my eyes telling my friend.

She hugged me hard and said, "Go get him; what you are waiting
for?"

"How am I looking today?" I asked my friends.

"*Stunningly beautiful!* He will die there and then only when he
will look at you."

"Please come along to the stairs with me." I asked for help from
my friends.

They were all excited to meet Nikhil. And with my friends, I went
to the terrace. There they stayed back and I stepped on the terrace. It
was all dark with a table, and a candle lit on it just like a perfect date.
My seniors had helped him to create this ambience. As I took my
first step on the terrace, I shouted his name "Nikhil" to attract his
attention.

He was dressed up in a black tuxedo borrowed from one of my
seniors, and I knew he was here to propose to me.

He turned back. He looked like a perfect gentleman with a rose in her hand. And yes it was a red rose I was dying to receive from him. He smiled at me, and I could imagine a million stars twinkling in his eyes. *"Oh My God!"* He was here for me whereas I had never ever told him my real name. With the reference of a fake name, he had found me.

He came close to me, and we shook hands. He then kissed on my hand and offered me a seat like a true gentle man. He looked like a dream which had come true. I had never felt so lucky. I took my seat while he knelt and offered me the red flower which he had for me, and I could not resist it. I was all crying from inside, and Nikhil was just smiling. I was feeling shy, and my heart was pounding fast.

"How did you find me Nikhil?" I was curious to know. **"With a journey from Kota to Kangra and then here to your University."** he kept smiling as he took his seat in front of me.

"But am destined to somewhere else" he continued, yet so pure; I felt shy.

"And how did you manage to enter my University?" I questioned him again.

"Just broke into here. It's a long story, but today it's only you, and because I had a lot of questions to ask," he replied.

"You did all this for me?" I asked him again as I could not believe him sitting in front of me.

"All for you Pari," he replied and the smile was still there on his face.

"But why?"

"Because as you left me; one day I came to realize that I love you," he looked straight into my eyes, and the eye contact remained there for the next two minutes.

I too kept looking into his eyes to find the truth. He found me with no clues. It was enough for me. I could not believe he was saying it to me and then found that we both, we both were crying for each other.

"What?" I asked him.

"I want to propose to you," he looked so silly but cute. "You really want to know my answer?" I asked him.

"Ya"

"I don't know what to say you are a writer, and I am a simple girl, I would have said it to you long ago, but I think there is no match."

"I am here just to know the answer nothing else," he went straight to the point.

"I know you believe a little less in love because of your past relationship and so do I" he continued.

"But when I was with you, I was complete, and you know I am tired of caring, and now I want to be cared for."

He kept on as if something was stuck in his heart and this was something he had to confess. It was the pain he had gone through to find me all the way from one side of the country. I kept mum to give him a chance to confess what he had in his heart.

"I am tired of loving, I want to get loved. I am tired of being called, I want to be called, we" he continued looking into my eyes romantically.

"I want to know your answer; as you complete me."

"I want to be us. But where to start that it will then never end."

"Are you proposing to me Niks?" I asked.

"*Oh! GOD* if it's not love then what is it, why I am here?" he replied.

"What in this world can I do for you to believe in love again and have you in my life?" he continued.

"**IT'S SIMPLE YOU WILL WRITE A BOOK FOR ME AS YOU WROTE FOR PRIYA**" I gave a tricky option.

"**ONLY IF YOU WILL CO-AUTHOR IT WITH ME**" he smiled back hugging me.

"**I love you Pari,**" said Nikhil to me; as our lips met.

And by the way, my name is **Aakhyaa**" I smiled back kissing him passionately.

"But for me you are Pari; my angel." and we kissed each other for the next five minutes under the beautiful moon.

I then sat on the terrace with him. Suddenly something struck, my mind; I asked "You said you are destined to somewhere else? Where?"

"Yes, I think I am destined into your arms" and then we hugged under the moon.

Few months later

Rings

"Hello" as I pick up my phone.

"Congratulations; our book got selected, and I am in a course to get it published," Nikhil jumped with excitement. I could easily find it out.

"When? And did you decide any title?" I inquired.

"Yeah," he answered.

"What?" I was curious to know it.

He revealed:

"A little love Incident… and accidently a love story"
Based on real-life events*

My Love never facked...

As Long as I Love you...

www.ingramcontent.com/pod-product-compliance
Lightning Source LLC
Chambersburg PA
CBHW060121260626
47160CB00005B/1963